# THE LIFE AND OPINIONS
# OF ZACHARIAS LICHTER

MATEI CALINESCU (1934–2009), born and educated in
Romania, was one of the leading intellectuals of his generation.
His novel *The Life and Opinions of Zacharias Lichter* (published
in Romanian in 1969) acquired cult status among generations
of young people despite attempts by Romanian authorities to
expunge Calinescu's name and works from cultural memory. He
emigrated to America in 1973 and established himself in his new
homeland as a literary scholar, publishing his two major works,
*Five Faces of Modernity* (1977; ultimately translated into eight
languages) and *Rereading* (1993), and teaching in the Comparative Literature Department at Indiana University. After the
collapse of Ceauşescu's national-Communist dictatorship in
1989, Calinescu was welcomed once more in his home country.
In a poll of literary critics conducted there in 2001, *The Life and
Opinions of Zacharias Lichter* was ranked among the top ten
Romanian prose works of the twentieth century. A sixteen-
volume edition of his selected literary and scholarly works is
currently in progress.

ADRIANA CALINESCU is the Thomas T. Solley curator
emerita of ancient art at Indiana University's Eskenazi Museum
of Art. She has written widely on the subject of ancient art and
is the editor of the scholarly work *Ancient Jewelry and Archaeol-
ogy*. She has translated works from English into Romanian,

including Mary Shelley's *Frankenstein*, which is the standard text in Romania.

BREON MITCHELL is a professor emeritus of Germanic studies and comparative literature at Indiana University. A past president of the American Literary Translators Association, he has received numerous national awards for literary translations, including the Helen and Kurt Wolff Prize, the Aldo and Jeanne Scaglione Prize from the Modern Language Association, and the Schlegel-Tieck Prize from the British Society of Authors. His translations from the German include Franz Kafka's *The Trial* and Günter Grass's *The Tin Drum*, as well as works by Heinrich Böll, Siegfried Lenz, Uwe Timm, and Marcel Beyer.

NORMAN MANEA has written numerous books of fiction and nonfiction, including the memoir *The Hooligan's Return* and the novel *The Lair*. He has been awarded several literary prizes, including the MacArthur Fellowship, the Guadalajara International Book Fair's (FIL) 2016 Literature in Romance Languages Award, and the Prix Médicis étranger. He is a professor emeritus and Distinguished Writer in Residence at Bard College.

# THE LIFE AND OPINIONS OF ZACHARIAS LICHTER

MATEI CALINESCU

*Translated from the Romanian by*
**ADRIANA CALINESCU** *and*
**BREON MITCHELL**

*Introduction by*
**NORMAN MANEA**

NEW YORK REVIEW BOOKS

*New York*

THIS IS A NEW YORK REVIEW BOOK
PUBLISHED BY THE NEW YORK REVIEW OF BOOKS
435 Hudson Street, New York, NY 10014
www.nyrb.com

Library of Congress Cataloging-in-Publication Data
Names: Calinescu, Matei author. | Calinescu, Adriana, 1941– translator |
  Mitchell, Breon translator
Title: The life and opinions of Zacharias Lichter / Matei Calinescu ; translated
  from the Romanian by Adriana Calinescu and Breon Mitchell ; introduction
  by Norman Manea.
Other titles: Viața și opiniile lui Zacharias Lichter. English
Description: New York : New York Review Books, 2018. | Series: New York
  Review Books classics
Identifiers: LCCN 2017048228 (print) | LCCN 2017046079 (ebook) | ISBN
  9781681371955 (paperback) | ISBN 9781681371962 (epub)
Subjects: LCSH: Romanians—Fiction. | BISAC: FICTION / Historical. |
  FICTION / Jewish. | GSAFD: Biographical fiction | Historical fiction
Classification: LCC PC840.13.A39 V5313 2018 (ebook) | LCC PC840.13.A39
  (print) | DDC 859/.334—dc23
LC record available at https://lccn.loc.gov/2017048228

ISBN 978-1-68137-195-5
Available as an electronic book; ISBN 978-1-68137-196-2

Printed in the United States of America on acid-free paper.
10  9  8  7  6  5  4  3  2  1

# CONTENTS

# INTRODUCTION

*THE LIFE and Opinions of Zacharias Lichter* was first published in Communist Romania in 1969. It was surprising that such an unusual book should have come out at all under the repressive Ceauşescu regime, but then the late 1960s saw a brief period of relative liberalization, and the book, not obviously political, appears to have confused the vigilance of the censors. Four years later, in 1973, as the Ceauşescu dictatorship reverted to brutal totalitarian form, the book's author, Matei Calinescu, left for America on a Fulbright Fellowship, abandoning his homeland and his career there as a university professor and a well-regarded man of letters (besides *Zacharias Lichter*, he was the author of several books of criticism and poetry). He settled with his family in Bloomington, Indiana, and was appointed a professor of comparative literature at Indiana University. After Calinescu went into exile, *Zacharias Lichter* disappeared from sight in Romania, circulating only in samizdat, now taken to be, as Professor Liviu Papadima has written in a 2013 festschrift for the author, "a highly subversive work," and indeed in his view, the regime was not entirely wrong. Papadima sees the book as "an uncanny apparition, a direct response to the political situation in Romania."

Another Romanian, the famous nihilist and exile Emil Cioran, has by contrast described *The Life and Opinions of*

*Zacharias Lichter* rather differently, as "a Baal Shem Tov imagined by Sterne." That's another way to look at this refined and challenging book, whose title does of course invite comparison to Laurence Sterne's *The Life and Opinions of Tristram Shandy*.

Who is Zacharias Lichter, that he inspires such complex, changing, and contradictory responses? A peaceful, mystical iconoclast, religious, it seems, but with no religious affiliation, who is also a curious and skeptical observer of the human spectacle of Bucharest, where he lives. Zacharias comes from a Jewish family; his father, Moses, is the owner of a small shop on Philanthropy Boulevard, on the outskirts of the capital. As a child, Zacharias was sent out with his brothers and sisters to peddle odds and ends on the street, until one evening, finding himself "enveloped by a divine flame," he hands out all his petty wares to passersby for free. His family is too shocked to know what to do, though they do relieve Zacharias of further chores. Later, while studying at the university (Zacharias is an excellent student and even submits a dissertation on Plotinus, though he neglects to pick up his diploma), he cuts off ties to his family altogether. Utterly rejecting the world of work, the ugly, ragged Zacharias leads a vagrant life and begs for a living. He writes poems but throws them away. He gives voice to cryptic aphorisms and cutting ironies. He clowns around. He is a kind of burlesque star of the vagabonds.

Zacharias has a number of companions. There is Leopold Nacht, Poldy, his "only true friend," a terminal alcoholic who "does not say a word" and whom Lichter considers "one of the great philosophers of contemporary Europe," an exponent of "a philosophy of designification" in which "the world ... must be emptied of sense, [since] only then will it become one with Being." Then there is another drunk, "who displays all the features of an aggressive thug," known in the bars as the Poet, and who is in fact a prolific author of pornographic verse. Zacharias respects him as "the annihilator of myths." Other characters include the ever reticent G., an intransigent moralist, expositor of the dialectics of "*suavizare*," and Doctor S., a psychiatrist, whose attentions fill Lichter with terror.

These figures, and others, alongside Lichter himself, come and go throughout the pages of Calinescu's book. Perhaps more important than any of them, however, is "humanity's first tragic hero," the biblical Job, credited with discovering the absurd and that "without God the absurd cannot exist." Lichter may seem a poor lonely wandering oddball, but he is also said to be a prophet, even if he hardly prophesizes. And bear in mind that Matei Calinescu has written elsewhere that "prophetic utterance comes into being via negation: it is knowledge induced by ashes.... Prophets feel the ashes of the world on their tongue."

*The Life and Opinions of Zacharias Lichter* is set in the 1930s, a significant and troubled period in modern Romanian history. Both nationalist extremism and anti-Semitism were growing, and the Iron Guard, a fanatical Christian-Orthodox movement that promoted a suprematist vision of a pure and glorious Romanian ethnicity and faith, was a powerful and terrorizing presence. The Iron Guard incited pogroms and sought to promulgate racial laws, paving the way for the country's later military alliance with Nazi Germany. They acted under the banner of what they called hooliganism, an ideology claimed to have been taken from the work of Mihai Eminescu (1850–1889), the greatest of Romanian poets and, in the Iron Guard's view, the patron saint of hooligans.

And indeed the literary world was involved in the political developments of the time. Many important intellectuals and writers actively supported or were at least sympathetic to the extreme right. Mircea Eliade, not yet famous as a historian of religion, is a notorious example. In Eliade's novel *Huliganii* (The Hooligans, 1935) a character who is evidently the author's mouthpiece lauds "the hooliganic experience. Don't respect anything, don't believe in anything except your youth, your biology.... Who doesn't start like this, toward himself and toward the world—will not create anything. To forget all the truths, to have such vitality in yourself as to be immune from and not intimidated by truth,—this is, in fact, the calling for a hooligan."

Eliade sets up the hooligan as the exemplary opponent of a despised "bourgeois morality," a dreamer and a willing martyr devoted to the great sacred cause of purifying the homeland of foreigners and freethinkers, allowing it at last to stand "as clear as the moon in the sky."

The year before Eliade's novel came out, the Jewish writer Mihail Sebastian, until recently his friend, published a novel of his own, *For Two Thousand Years*, which described from a personal point of view the growth of Romanian anti-Semitism. Sebastian asked Nae Ionescu, a former professor and mentor at the university, to write a preface to the book, and Ionescu, having become a fanatical right-wing Christian nationalist ideologue in the interim, responded with a harshly polemical and defamatory text that Sebastian nonetheless felt obliged to publish. The book and the preface provoked a huge political and literary scandal. Sebastian was attacked by both the right and the left; in the Jewish community he was accused of duplicity and even complicity with his adversaries. To all this Sebastian responded with a brilliant essay entitled "How I Became a Hooligan," in which he envisions a very different kind of hooligan from Eliade. Sebastian's hooligan is a solitary outsider, always "a dissident, never a partisan," "a man in a jacket, not a uniform," no militant but a skeptic and an independent thinker, believing not in the collective but only in the individual.

Zacharias Lichter may be said to be a hooligan in this sense, but also in another, distinctly political sense the word took on under Ceauşescu's Communist dictatorship. In Ceauşescu's brutal totalitarian state—with its generalized suspicion and ubiquitous surveillance and mandatory demonstrations of obedience, with its endless cynical and demagogic displays of phony patriotic euphoria, those parades and political meetings full of childish songs and slogans—anybody who lacked an ID and work papers was legally designated a hooligan and as such was subject to persecution and even arrest. And soon, as I have described in my book *The Hooligan's Return* (2003), this poisonous state-imposed "identity" was broadened to include a host of undesirables, rootless cosmopolitans, religious believers, former owners of factories, banks, of land, citizens of "suspect" ethnicity, people in touch with Western relatives or journalists, independent thinkers, and needless to say any open adversaries of the system. Certainly Zacharias Lichter would have been among them.

When a third edition of *Zacharias Lichter* was published in 1995, after the fall of the Ceauşescu regime, Calinescu added a preface in which he discussed his reason for setting the book in the 1930s. It was, he admits, a dodge to mislead the censors, and he speaks with shame and guilt about having had to censor himself; one of the main reasons for his difficult decision to choose exile was to escape that burden. And yet Calinescu's comments on his own book are nuanced:

> If this book is a historical document, then it is not only by what it's saying but also by what it's not saying, I would like to believe, by its eloquent silence, by what is absent in the furious speeches of this prophet, by his silent revolt, no less intense than his ardent words; not only is he asocial but he sees in his choice an expression of a moral revolt and a way of salvation.

In the book, Calinescu emphasizes that Lichter's God is one of nonexistence, his theology one of apophasis, in which the divine is manifested only through negation. The end of religion, he affirms, is nothing less than perplexity. Not far from a spiritual hooligan, we may say.

Some of Lichter's sayings, in the excellent translation by Adriana Calinescu and Breon Mitchell:

> I may be afraid of dogs and butterflies, but I would throw myself on the pyre at any time for an idea.

> Acrobats have replaced saints.

> Modern civilization [is] a vast extension of the Realm of Stupidity... sure of itself, economical, [with] wide-spreading technological tentacles... the domain of stupidity is progress itself....

[M]oney... must be given to real beggars, to cripples dragging themselves along the street, to old vagabonds, to the blind, to gypsies.

[The] strident trumpets of clowns unleash the *apocalypse*...work becomes one of the ways by which the category of *to have* absorbs that of *to be.*... [The] prophet... expounded on his grand concept of social utopia: the overthrow of the capitalist system through the conversion of millions of workers to begging and the founding of a new society, religious and anarchic, where ownership, though not banned by law, would become a form of alienation, a shameful illness... (... quarantined in luxurious leper-hospitals....)

Blessed be the flame that is ravaging my being,
the flame that ignites my dry words,
the flame that ignites even my perishable shadow,
the flame of anguish and joy,
the terrible flame of God.

I, the prophet-clown; I, the beggar... I myself have been *chosen*—God *chose* me—to answer for all the mistakes, past, present, and future, of my fellow creatures.

That this hooligan and provocateur should attract the attention of the secret police, be they those of the reactionary 1930s or of Ceauşescu's Securitate, is hardly surprising.

Zacharias Lichter is, in his peaceful way, the enemy of any social consensus, of any given social order. Calinescu's book has survived thanks to its ambiguities and its refined and clear style, which stands in drastic contrast to the "wooden language" of the official press of his day. It survives too because the things it describes survive. Aren't we witnessing nowadays the systematization and spreading of countless modes of lying?

Though the bleak bloody parody may appear to be unending, Lichter remains a disciple of Spinoza. Salvation is to be found not thanks to some faraway god or in the afterlife but in the here and now, in human beings and the vitality of nature.

—NORMAN MANEA

# THE LIFE AND OPINIONS
# OF ZACHARIAS LICHTER

# PORTRAIT

MANY WHO chance to see him now and then, if only in passing, recognize him at once from the briefest of descriptions: a strange creature, so ludicrously ugly he produces a strong impression on even the indifferent observer—leaving behind one of those liminal but nagging memories that remain concealed in the shadows, only to surge forth from time to time with incredible freshness and precision.

Haunting our streets and parks for year after year, his thick and twisted body clothed in squalid beggar's rags, almost ostentatiously bizarre in his behavior, he has become one of the city's most familiar and picturesque figures, one whose prolonged absence would no doubt be noted and even remarked upon with nostalgia. Too few of us know, however, that this exterior conceals the fiery personality of one of the last descendants of the ancient race of great prophets. In fact, viewed more closely, the distorted features that make him a local character lose their picturesque qualities and suggest instead an enigmatic mixture of the angelic and the monstrous, arousing in more delicate souls a sense of unease akin to anxiety.

Zacharias Lichter has, as he himself likes to say, the physiognomy of a metaphysician, an enlightened late-eighteenth-century German Jew—with irregularities and deformities bordering on the grotesque. His swollen, asymmetrical face,

pushed forward forcefully by prominent cheekbones, re-
calls—in its moments of repose—a hieratic totem mask,
coarsely molded by rude and clumsy hands trembling with
sacred terror. And it must be said that among the first impressions Zacharias Lichter awakens is a particularly strong
sense of fierce, irrepressible vigor. This may be due in part
to his highly developed pilary system, manifest both in his
thick and prickly black beard and in the abundant hairs
springing from the nostrils of his peerless Semitic nose, as
well as the wiry entanglement of chest hair peeping through
gaps in his shirt where buttons are missing. Although the
crown of his large head reveals an extensive bald spot of a
matte brown that makes it seem calcified, locks of hair blaze
forth around it like black flames of fire.

What a hasty observer may simply consider slipshod attire
(his ancient and discolored tattered coat; his rumpled and
patched trousers with their frayed cuffs; his scorched and
misshapen shoes—seemingly saved from some conflagration
and molded by long wear to the knotty shape of his feet)
reflects not so much the social sense of poverty as its Platonic
idea. Lichter strives to embody this condition as a further
symbol of the inner state of a prophet touched by God's
flame. The eternal glow of that flame, at times distant and
faint, at others fierce and blinding, seems to explain both
Zacharias Lichter's constant blinking (his eyes, with their
short, sparse, ash-hued lashes, blink often and rapidly) and
the earthen tinge of his coarse, puffy skin.

Far from viewing all this as something shameful, or as
some mysterious punishment, as one might expect, Zacharias
Lichter is proud of his ugliness and interprets it as a sign of
divine election, which from time to time, to preserve its true
purity, is imprinted with gruesome stigmata. ("Angels"—he

says—"feel the need to hide in a monster's cesspool now and then.")

For those who know him, Zacharias Lichter's most striking peculiarity remains his manner of speech, which lessens and sometimes annuls the effect of his physical deformities. Words burst from his mouth in torrents, accompanied by miming motions and the disturbingly wild gesticulations exhibited by madmen determined at all costs to convince their listeners. In Lichter's case, however, the motivation is quite different: his entire being is partaking in the violent effort of expression, as if imbued with the necessity of *saying*.

Especially mesmerizing are his hands, which cast rapid signs in the air like a mysterious visual language. Touched at such times by the terrible flame of divine purity, swelling from its heat, his hands never draw back from its crackling blaze. As a matter of fact, the words Zacharias Lichter utters, the provoking stances he assumes (which often seem scandalously contradictory) and, in the final analysis, his entire existence, are nothing but a desperate attempt to translate into human terms—as he himself confesses—the experience of closeness to God: an *absurd* experience, filled with fear and ecstasy, painfully tearing one's being to pieces, only to reassemble it again, in a never-ending cycle.

# ON GOD'S FLAME

"NOT LONG ago, on a mild and clear afternoon, I was heading for a public garden, a morsel of bread in my pocket and a jar of yogurt in my hand"—Zacharias Lichter once recounted to friends. "I was tired and hungry and couldn't wait to sit down on a bench and start eating. In my absent-minded state I didn't notice a crack gaping at me from the asphalt sidewalk: I stumbled, fell, and the yogurt jar smashed to smithereens, spattering my clothes. As if my plight weren't ludicrous enough, I began shouting and thrashing about, inexplicably terror stricken, as if I had fallen into an abyss instead of onto the ground. The scene would not have been perfect without the presence of passersby. There they were, giggling and pointing at me, gathering about in an amused circle. The moment I came to my senses, still on the sidewalk, I rejected with angry stubbornness the commonsense arguments that rushed to reconstruct a chain of events resulting in my present position: flat on the ground, yogurt spattered, and clasping the broken jar in my hand.

"Suddenly, the true cause of my terror dawned on me with the utmost clarity: I had been struck by God's flame! Its flash had blinded me, striking me like a stone, deafening me with its roar, parching my mouth with heat, and leaving behind a terrible thirst. I picked myself up, trembling and unsteady, while those around me drew back in apparent fear:

my face must have seemed a grotesque and menacing mask. But I was oblivious to their presence, for I could still hear the terrifying roar of God's flame rattling the canopy of the world. Suddenly, people began turning into strange creatures before my eyes: I was stumbling through swine-snouted figures, humans with the heads of eagles, frogs, and rats. Children emitted incredibly high-pitched tones from huge lily-like corollas that grew in lieu of their heads. Creatures kept surging past: half human, half dog or goat, people with the flickering forked tongues of snakes. And above it all, the steady reverberation of God's plunging flame. I walked on aimlessly until, with an automatic gesture, I mopped my brow, which was dripping with sweat, blurring my vision, and weariness overwhelmed me. I felt hungry again. Beast-headed people were appearing less frequently. Now I had to walk some distance, and on crowded streets, to chance upon one or two. At last, toward evening, things returned to their natural order; visions and hallucinations vanished. God's flame now burned from afar, in silence."

# ON THE STAGES OF THE SPIRITUAL

FOR KIERKEGAARD'S famous stages—the aesthetic, the ethical, and the religious—Zacharias Lichter substitutes the hierarchy *circus—madness—perplexity*. Spiritual life—he maintains—inevitably develops in terms of one of these existential categories.

Circus—the lowest stage of the spiritual—may be expressed as an awareness of the absurd spectacle of our existence. Reduced to the figure of a clown, forced to play a humiliatingly vulgar role, suffering and rebelling against his state, yet knowing he can never overcome it, realizing that all his efforts will be in vain, such is the man who lives beneath the coarse canvas panoply of the world as circus. His suffering and his revolt can only be expressed through irony. With his frenetic clowning, meant to unleash unbridled laughter, the clown implicates, by means of this painfully lucid irony, the whole of mankind. The more exaggerated and grotesque his role, the more vividly he sees himself as an embodiment of the human condition. Circus, as the first stage of the spiritual, means abandoning oneself to the demon of irony. It is the triumph of parody: pathos turns somersaults in the arena's sawdust; weeping engenders an echoing laughter and in so doing renders all things infinitely trivial. Slowly, imperceptibly, under his floury mask furrowed by fake tears, the clown moves toward a tragic state beyond the immediate and the contingent, an ontological state rooted in loneliness and dumb silence. In the hierarchy of the spiritual, the final lesson of circus is unspoken and ineffable. It is only revealed, with all its hidden meanings, to those who understand the necessity to soil, to demean, to trample *communication* beneath their feet.

All people are clowns—Zacharias Lichter maintains—yet few achieve a metaphysical knowledge of their condition. Of those lucid-minded clowns who do, even fewer take up the vocation of spiritual madness. (To be sure, the madness Zacharias Lichter refers to is a concept based, like that of circus, on metaphor. Yet that metaphor retains a disturbingly ambiguous relationship to pathological alienation.) Any form of consciousness, no matter how limited, implies duality: madness is unification. It seems that the more acutely people suffer from the painful contradictions of their conscious mind, the stronger is their *longing for madness*. For madness alone can break through the oppressively conventional nature of all languages, the arbitrary sign systems by means of which those struggling to communicate are led to adhere to increasingly complex structures foreign to their deepest being.

Clowns realize that languages are abstract constructs and thus mock them, assaulting them by means of the comic. The insane, as in a dream, establish magical connections between words and objects; for them, symbols become palpable and real, endowed with hallucinatory strength. Madness, in spiritual life, implies living in myth, in a mythic *chaos*. It is moreover a secret protest against a world alienated from the spiritual, against the world of the immediate and habitual. Only the mad can fill the void of the pathetic with content. For is there anything more pathetic than to live in a world of truth and have an alienated world reject you as alien; to live in the sphere of the serious and have a ludicrous world laugh at you because it finds you ludicrous?

The mad can fall, though only rarely, into perplexity. Prophecy, asceticism, prayer, even great poetry are forms of madness in spiritual life. Consciously or not they tend towards the abyss of perplexity, but more often than not, without losing themselves in it. In perplexity—Zacharias Lichter maintains—all perception dissolves as the very sense organs that allow us to register the appearance of reality are suspended, as if in a state of paralysis. From darkness, from silence, from the void, from the atemporal and aspatial, divinity draws its spirit, revealing itself through negation and absence.

A brief analysis of the notions of *darkness* and *silence* will contribute to an understanding of what Zacharias Lichter means by *perplexity*. The nature of darkness can, he says, be inferred with reference to the infirmity of the blind. Unlikely as it may seem, we are all more or less capable of replicating the actual experience of those who cannot see. The blind— Zacharias Lichter contends—are mistakenly believed to be plunged in total darkness. In fact, darkness is a visual sensation that presupposes the existence of visual perception but the absence of a visual stimulus, in this case, the absence of light. I can represent the kind of darkness in which the blind live by instead concentrating my attention on all that lies at a given moment outside my field of vision. For example, I am looking out the window and see the barren trees, the succession of roofs, the leaden sky. And suddenly, by an act of the conscious mind, I can see what, at this precise moment, is not part of my visual field, what lies, let us say, behind my back and could not be actualized in terms of vision. The awareness of the extravisual, extended to an awareness of the nonvisual, can give rise to an intuition of what darkness is for the blind, and this awareness is accessible to anyone, plus or minus a coefficient of approximation. In the stage of perplexity, darkness becomes absolute and God himself drifts within it. We can remark similarly on the essence of silence, which should not be identified with the absence of sound (an auditory phenomenon) but with all that takes place outside the auditory sphere and is impossible to represent in terms of hearing. The absence of noise is an experience of those who can hear. True silence is an experience of the deaf. In the stage of perplexity, this silence takes on an absolute and revelatory character.

In some sense we could say that Zacharias Lichter is an adherent of the disturbing theology of apophasis, according to which God can only be known *via negationis*, as a *non-existens, non-ens*, as *nihil*. The difference for Zacharias Lichter is that this theoretical knowledge of the divine is justifiable only if one has experienced Perplexity. Without that experience, such knowledge remains a simple speculative exercise, ingenious but sterile.

# FROM THE POEMS OF
# ZACHARIAS LICHTER

A clown played the trumpet: ta-ra-ra-ta-ra-ra-ta-ra-ra
monsters coupled with angels
like huge frogs coupling with drowned children's souls
a choir of youths intoned in the rain-colored air
the hymn of exfoliated lilies
worms writhed towards the inaccessible pyres of Ecstasy
ta-ra-ra-ta-ra-ra played on
the trumpet of the blind thousand-year-old clown

Suddenly the onrush of madmen opened the festival of
    Freedom
the tongue of sand rock and rivers
the tongue of snakes and golden-chinned lizards
asserted itself as the tongue of universal wisdom
the old hoarse ta-ra-ra-ta-ra-ra
of the clown's trumpet was fading away
the choir fainter and fainter

Among the madmen some were falling
as their ears became leaves
their fingers thinned to white roots
their bones turned to heavy stone and their eyes melted to
    rivulets of water
in the bosom of the deep night of Being

But the ta-ra-ra-ta-ra-ra
of the clown's trumpet burst forth again at dawn
and the monsters rushed once more into the pure
silence of the angels
ta-ra-ra-ta-ra-ra

# ON THE BOOK OF JOB

DURING Jewish lent, which he scrupulously observes (subjecting himself to the pangs of hunger and especially *thirst*, for he sees in thirst the *bodily form* of prayer), Zacharias Lichter reads from the Old Testament. The book to which he returns most often is that of Job, long passages of which he knows by heart and comments upon with stern fervor.

Job, says Zacharias Lichter, is humanity's first tragic hero and the only one who played out that tragedy to its very end, for he discovered the *absurd* and at the same time *necessary* core of suffering. The dialogue between rigorous innocence and the destructive flame of purity is, after all, the only fundamentally tragic circumstance: all the rest is merely barren babble.

God makes a bet with Satan, and the absurd strikes Job down—since suffering is only the outer skin, the rotting flesh of a fruit that already holds the germinating seed of the absurd. Will Job curse God, as seems logical to Satan (who thus affirms the principle of all practical morality based on *do ut des*)? No, because Job's logic is of a different nature, infinitely deeper and much simpler: he yearns for death, he curses the day he was born, he doubts the justice of the world. He revolts, in a word, against his absurd destiny. But not for a moment does he fall prey to the strange, truly devastating force of the curse and deny the One who has crushed him beneath the weight of Calamity. He does not because he is *pure*; because deprived of its absurd kernel (the paradoxical gift of Goodness), his suffering would have consisted merely of endless horror, a disgusting rottenness; because his silence *afterwards* would have filled his mouth with all the world's waste; because he would have condemned himself to eternal nausea and reduced his existence, for ages to come, to endless spasms of perpetual vomiting. Job obscurely knows that without God the absurd cannot exist. He also knows that, without the absurd, purity dies, revolt gives way to disgust, truth to abject lie, and repentance—that miracle—to boundless boredom.

The Book of Job contains a *morality of the absurd*, and everything that Job suffers is an *initiation* into that morality. Conventional moral principles (generally compensatory) are rejected from the outset. In a polemic suffused with authentic suffering, Job rebukes the specious arguments of the three friends who come to comfort him in his adversity: Eliphaz the Temanite, Bildad the Shuhite, and Zophar the Naamathite. Theirs is the hypocritical discourse that attempts to justify suffering: God punishes those guilty of sin, even if it was involuntary, and we must accept our plight with resignation; suffering never strikes the truly innocent; God acts according to principles of justice the essence of which man cannot fathom; man must come to terms with his prescribed lot, and so on.

But Job confounds all such sophisms: he is blameless and upright, no sin stains his conscience, yet a terrible and absurd affliction has befallen him, an injustice so great it threatens the very stability of the world … And behold, God speaks to Job. And Job does not fall silent: he *questions* God, he *defends himself*, he *revolts* against God, and finally he *obeys*, filled with repentance and self-hatred. And God, the creator of mankind, *admits Job is right, suffuses with truth* what Job has said, and turns in anger against Eliphaz the Temanite and his companions ... Because in the realm of human understanding, Logos can exist only in the Absurd.

Every time he talks about Job, Zacharias Lichter is transfigured; his eyes grow wild and his thirst-parched lips take on the reddish tinge of fire or blood.

# ON COURAGE

"BY TEMPERAMENT"—Zacharias Lichter confessed one day—"I am anxious, obsessive and even cowardly. Under circumstances that elicit no reaction whatsoever in a normal person, a wave of physical fear makes me lose my senses. For instance, when I see dogs, those vagabond dogs with eyes that gleam with infinite kindness, tragic dogs capable—they say—of committing suicide, I am seized by an uncontrollable, violent, and at times paralyzing terror. I start howling, I flee (to the astonishment of passersby) like a man possessed, or I freeze in a mindless catatonic state, staring at them rigidly. I once stood in the middle of the street for almost an hour that way—it was a hot, dry summer, reeking of melting asphalt. The dog was wagging its tail, sniffing at me, while I stood transfixed, unable to make the slightest gesture or the faintest sound."

Were Zacharias Lichter not leading an exclusively urban existence, his excessive fear of dogs would no doubt extend to other animals: oxen or river buffalos, billy goats, or rams—his hyperbolic imagination would detect signs of a terrifying potential for aggression in all of them. Even so, Lichter's propensity for fear seems fully justified: various insects—wasps, bumblebees, honeybees, beetles—not to mention moths or bats which, as evening descends on the park, seem to have a predilection for colliding with the philosopher's brightly bulging forehead—all of these, enlarged tenfold by the diopter of fear in Lichter's eyes, are transformed into fabulous creatures. Threatening, endowed with Cyclopean eyes and monstrous rattling wings, they seem ready to plunge their venomous stingers into his body or dust him with poisonous pollen.

"The ridicule I provoke"—Lichter admits—"arises from the huge discrepancy between the elevated spiritual level at which my courage reveals itself and the basic physiological level of my terror. But it is a sublime state of ridicule! I may be afraid of dogs and butterflies, but I would throw myself on the pyre at any time for an idea. I would not hesitate to be a guinea pig for a scientist testing a new drug—against cancer, say. But indiscriminate courage reveals a want of imagination and ultimately a form of imbecility.

"The senseless bravura of a champion race-car driver, or of a man scaling the terrifying rock face of a mountain against a stopwatch, seem to me forms of spiritual alienation based on the *intoxication of risk*. For courage involves not simple and gratuitous daring, but responsibility. Modern societies tend to eschew responsibility, at least as a factor in human interaction, and replace it with the manifold and diverse forms of the cult of risk-taking. But in risk only the mechanics of courage, emptied of any content, are retained. The main accent falls on the game, on competition, on a show of skill and strength. Conceived in this way, courage loses all its grandeur: instead of expressing the martyr's inflexible free will, it displays the dexterity (dangerous, indeed) of a trapeze artist. Acrobats have replaced saints. In fact, fear and courage are only apparently contradictory. Even the most timorous person may display amazing courage, in the noble sense that should be restored to this notion. Fear is but a natural reaction in face of risk (bravery being its opposite); on the other hand, courage means incorporating a categorical imperative and presupposes transcending risk in spiritual terms. Being a Christian during the declining years of the Roman Empire meant courage, not just assuming risks. Even if it was objectively present—as was fear—risk was totally unimportant and utterly risible in comparison with the sublime altitude of courage. My temperament is fearful but my spirit breathes the pure air of courage."

# ON THE REALM OF STUPIDITY

IN ORDER to grasp Lichterian thought it is essential to understand his conception of stupidity. He sees it as mimicry, because stupidity apes—at all levels—intelligence, sometimes so faithfully that even astute minds mistake one for the other. Nothing is further from the truth than the belief that stupidity has its own, recognizable stamp: on the contrary, it is astonishingly varied, capable of morphing into the most diverse and unpredictable forms. Its vulgar hypostases aside, one can say—as paradoxical as it sounds—that by assimilating the discoveries of intelligence and by mimicking its manifestations, stupidity contributes to the progress of humanity. The rare and brilliant act of creativity becomes a "fiscal gain," a source of profit, exploited with patience and deftness. Stupidity is tenacious, accumulative, and applicative, acting as a mode of inertia: it ensures the circulation of ideas and values.

No wonder then that Lichter sees modern civilization as a vast extension of the Realm of Stupidity. Intelligence is obsessed with that which is fundamental, original, structural, essential. One recognizes intelligent individuals by their fascination with the elementary and the simple. Their efforts within the spiritual order are integrative: they seek the basic principle, or—to put it metaphorically—the ideal key to all the mysteries of the world. Aspiring towards totality and uniqueness is not stupidity's ambition. Its strength lies in its ability to placidly accept any theory, even an erroneous one, as long as it offers a viable starting point towards practical results. A parasite plagiarizing the pure core of intelligence, sapping its vigor, stupidity forever fortifies and perfects itself, sprawling like a vast and dangerous stain on the consciousness of humanity. For stupidity is vain (the vanity of "efficiency"), sure of itself, economical, has wide-spreading technological tentacles and is shrewdly and ferociously aggressive. Stupidity wills itself to be "universally human." Since the domain of stupidity is progress itself, Zacharias Lichter naturally concludes that true intelligence evolves within a vicious circle, forever fantasizing escape yet forever falling back into the realization that all efforts at escape are futile.

# BEGGING

THE ONLY profession Zacharias Lichter practices on occasion—and this should come as no surprise—is begging. One may occasionally see this strange prophet seeking alms— he may well even show up in the city center—his face flushed, his gaze sparkling, his gestures awkward and humble, though secretly ironic. "Help a poor metaphysician," he says in the tone of voice one generally reserves for some terrible infirmity. Most passersby consider Zacharias Lichter mad and scuttle past in alarm; others rummage nervously through their pockets and hastily drop a coin or two into his outstretched hand, eager to lose sight of this strange figure whose insistence they sense as obscurely threatening. Still others—for Lichter begs from anyone, indiscriminately, without limiting himself to "easy touches"—mock him, or, confronted by such a robust beggar, raise "holy hell" and pelt him with the grossest of insults. (In such cases Lichter wears a saintly smile, and a flicker of beauty floats for a moment across his frightful face.) Begging—Zacharias Lichter assures us—is the profession that brings one closest to God. It is a form of self-preservation through perpetual self-denial; it is asceticism and at the same time the disdain of asceticism. Moreover, Lichter sees begging as one of the most efficacious means of self-knowledge. That is why, to his disciples—some of them young and leading lives devoid of any pecuniary concerns—he recommends begging as a purely spiritual exercise. In order for the circle to close perfectly, money thus gathered must be given to real beggars, to cripples dragging themselves along the street, to old vagabonds, to the blind, to gypsies.

A person structurally incapable of begging is, in Lichter's eyes, clearly condemned to mediocrity, spat forth with disgust from God's mouth, and impelled by the angels of fire and the angels of ice toward the gates of the vast Realm of Stupidity.

# EXISTENCE AND POSSESSION

ABSORBED as he is with the category of being—by virtue of the one freedom he recognizes as his own, that of embracing one's fate—Zacharias Lichter belongs to the rare breed that has overcome the spirit of possession, with all its deceptions and insidious tendencies. We can speak of his poverty as a *work* that can be understood only in relation to its ideal and perfect model, the Platonic *idea* of poverty. It would thus be mistaken to call Zacharias Lichter a *pauper*, to place him in a social category that permits relative comparisons. He is instead—excuse the cumbersome and awkward formulation—a *bearer of poverty*, understood here as an archetype and as a category (as a negation of *having*, because poverty is a mode of existence, a hypostasis of *being*); Lichter is not a pauper but an individual who partakes of the essence and genius of poverty, one who must be judged exclusively in terms of that essence.

From early adolescence on, Zacharias Lichter detached himself quite *naturally* from all he perceived as sullied by the secretly poisoned tentacles of *possession*. He started by distancing himself from his haberdasher family. (Moses Lichter, his father, kept a petty dry goods shop on Philanthropy Boulevard, where his family helped by carrying some of the merchandise in portable stalls to various city markets.)

As a child Zacharias helped in his father's shop and accompanied his older brothers and sisters as they peddled their motley goods. He even cried out wares in the street until his thin voice became hoarse and cracked—offering combs, buttons, shoelaces, soaps, or shoe polish. At around thirteen to fourteen years of age, left alone to mind the little stall one evening, Zacharias felt suddenly enveloped by a divine flame and, in a state of near delirium, gave away all the goods left in his care in less than a quarter of an hour. He gave without lifting his eyes, at random, to anyone who would accept his wares: to beggars, to children loitering in the market, even to those vagabonds who haunt crowded places in hope of some modest profit or, failing that, some opportunity for theft. Zacharias's act seemed so outlandish, so contrary to "nature," that his parents were unable to find a suitable punishment. Having no other real reason to complain of his son, a brilliant student whose sweet and open character was in total contrast to his ugliness (which made him even more lovable), *Domnul* Moses Lichter left the child unchastised and spared him any further involvement with the family's precarious trade. "An angel of fire came, and then, I don't know what happened . . ." Zacharias tried to explain.

Zacharias was around nineteen and a student of philosophy at the university when he left home and severed all ties with his family (although he never lost his affection for them). He moved into an abandoned garage on the outskirts of the city and made a living tutoring. He graduated with an outstanding dissertation on the *Enneads* of Plotinus but immediately withdrew from the circle of intellectual life, in spite of the numerous opportunities that awaited him there. He remained in occasional contact with only one or two of his former colleagues and visited his old professor of metaphysics once or twice a year to borrow books. The break was so complete that he did not even drop by to pick up his *licénce* diploma.

Illuminated and scorched by God's flame, Zacharias Lichter broke free from his past, inaugurating the cycle of his existence as a prophet with the discovery of the condition of the clown and its inherent irony. "I realized"—Lichter would later say—"that the strident trumpets of clowns unleash the *apocalypse*. I blew vigorously into countless colored-cardboard trumpets, initiating the festival of monsters and causing the great circus of the universe to roar: ta-ra-ra-ta-ra-ra-ta-ra-ra." At about this same time he discovered the deeper meaning of begging.

Zacharias Lichter's refusal to be gainfully employed should not be taken as a rejection of the *idea of work* itself, but as an expression of protest, a revolt against the possessive mentality that marks every constructive activity in our modern world. For working—Lichter explains—suddenly places you within a hierarchy. The place you hold within that hierarchy becomes your possession, which in turn presupposes accepting, even unwittingly, a system that defines you above all by your degree of participation in the sphere of *having* and only in a subsidiary sense in that of *being*, that is, in your own essence. Under such circumstances, work becomes one of the ways by which the category of *to have* absorbs that of *to be*. A tragic victim of betrayal and exploitation, the ordinary worker turns his *power to work* willy-nilly into a possession, which he constantly sells at a loss and rebuys only to sell again. And so it goes, on and on.

To prove that he was not opposed to the idea of work, but instead upheld it as one of the highest expressions of human nature (ontologically speaking, work is one of the forms of ecstasy), Zacharias Lichter plied several trades over a period of time—he learned masonry, welding, and at one point worked in a shop carving inscriptions on gravestones. Yet he stubbornly refused to accept any wages or other form of payment, and at the same time he continued begging while urging other workers to do the same. Conflicts were soon brewing. Although he was a zealous and productive worker, he quickly ran afoul of employers who took him for a loony, and a dangerous one at that, and gave him the sack. Many of his coworkers looked askance at this ugly, odd fellow who acted on incomprehensible ideas and principles and who refused to join in their *practical* solidarity by resorting to nebulous arguments couched in an otherworldly language. Others, laughing at Zacharias, though without malice, intuited in him an obscure force of self-denial and warm kindness. Partly for their own amusement and partly out of true empathy, they invited him into their homes. There the prophet (aware of course of how ridiculous he must have seemed) expounded on his grand concept of social utopia: the overthrow of the capitalist system through the conversion of millions of workers to begging and the founding of a new society, religious and anarchic, where ownership, though not banned by law, would become a form of alienation, a shameful illness, the object of revulsion and *pity*. ("Those infected by the ownership virus"—Zacharias Lichter passionately explained—"will be quarantined in luxurious leper-hospitals of the spirit, and future prophets and saints, as numerous as the workers of whom you are a part today, will *work* to support and care for them.") In the dramatic confusion of those years leading up to World War II, the bizarre behavior of Zacharias Lichter ultimately attracted the attention of security agencies, who suspected him of conducting dangerous political activity under the guise of religious mania. But no concrete evidence could be produced to support this suspicion.

Zacharias Lichter continued living a secluded life in the abandoned garage that had been his home since university years. This dilapidated shack was located in the back of a yard in which ramshackle mud huts sprouted like mushrooms around the unfinished building of the owner (an innkeeper, long bankrupt) whenever the sulky old man was forced to sell another patch of his land cheaply. Lichter had been allowed to sleep rent-free in the garage, which contained an ancient discarded couch. The unsightly figure of the prophet at first frightened the neighbors, especially the female contingent. (A scrawny sixteen-year-old girl, prone to hysterical outbursts, cried out "It's the devil!" the first time she saw him and took flight shrieking and crossing herself.) But as time went by most got used to his presence. Some would even help—with the direct and authentic simplicity of the humble—by bringing him an old coat of some kind, or sharing lunch or supper leftovers with him. The truth is that Lichter did not spend much time "at home." Summers he liked to sleep in parks, on the grass or behind a bush, or on a bench when the nights grew cooler. When he suffered from insomnia he would climb up a tree and, leaning back against a strong branch, meditate or pray. (One morning, seeing Zacharias perched in a blossoming linden tree, plunged in a state of semiwithdrawal, a surprised acquaintance called out to him, asking what he was doing up there. "I want to be closer to God," Lichter answered, closing his eyes and sinking again into silence.) In winter, when his garage was cold and the wind whistled through the cracks, he would sleep in waiting rooms at various railway stations until watchmen spotted him and chased him away. There were no objects of value in his abode except for a few books that he had borrowed. Only the Bible—an old edition with tiny letters printed on cheap, yellowing paper—was *his*. It had been given to him by a pious, simpleminded old woman, a neighbor to whom Zacharias Lichter spoke at times, in his usual torrential and abstract manner, about the terrifying flame of God.

In his constant striving toward the ideal, Zacharias Lichter managed little by little to turn his entire material existence into a vessel for the incorruptible essence of *poverty*. His condition therefore appears not as the result of social or psychological determinism but as a voluntary transcending of all (obvious or hidden) determinisms of possession through a spiritual act that lifts the immediate to the plenitude of *being*. Fully conscious that poverty is one of his most significant *works*, he sometimes says, not without a touch of humor: "My poverty is in itself a philosophical system worthy of a treatise."

# REGARDING THE DEVIL

"WHAT is the devil?" Zacharias Lichter was once asked. "First of all"—he replied—"the devil *is not*: he doesn't even try to *be*, realizing it's something he can never achieve. In keeping with a suggestion in Dostoyevsky, the devil strikes me as the symbolic embodiment of a mediocrity conscious of itself, of what we might call 'a mediocrity complex'—attaching, of course, an ontological sense to the psychological one. The devil illustrates the *impossibility of being*, as well as the awareness of that impossibility—the source of mediocrity in the universe. Metaphorically speaking, the devil is bathing in stale, lukewarm waters, prey to impotent anger at being forever excluded from the climate of extremes, furious that, even in this, he *cannot suffer*. Far from both ice and flame, the devil creates and destroys—simultaneously—all contingent rewards. He dreams all those timid and miserable dreams that will never be fulfilled, if only because he himself, by dreaming, mocks them...

"His existential failure fills the devil with a boundless resentment that is the source of the massive proliferating force of banality and mediocrity. To avenge his own *nonbeing*, the devil has founded the large and prosperous *Realm of Stupidity*. It is naive to consider the devil as the opposite of God (God can have no opposite but Himself), and it is just as naive to think of the devil as 'the spirit of negation,' since he is incapable of denying or affirming anything: all he can do is *put into practice*. Thus he is more properly identified with the 'practical spirit,' the very essence of stupidity. The devil lacks the aptitude to distinguish truth from falsehood. He is able, however, to distinguish with great accuracy between the possible and the impossible. Herein lies the terrible danger he represents, of which we must be constantly aware. In the realm of *practical* applications, possibilities are at least as rich for the false as for the true. Consequently, diabolical stupidity explores them with equal skill and perfect logic. In fact, the application of a false idea may yield more *practical results* than the application of a true one (since truth offers more resistance to such endeavors). Aren't we witnessing nowadays the systematization and spreading of countless modes of *lying*—in almost all domains of knowledge? Don't we see—what a disturbing phenomenon!—the fantastic speed at which innocent *errors*, under the meticulously organized actions of stupidity, turn into lies?"

Zacharias Lichter seemed frightened, his eyes glassy with uncharacteristic bewilderment.

"By persevering, full of resentment, in his own nonbeing"—he added—"the devil has chanced upon a terrifying discovery: the *power of lying*."

# DE AMICITIA

ZACHARIAS Lichter's only true friend is Leopold Nacht, a tall, gaunt man with a hobbling gait, whose head, albeit small, seems an overly heavy burden for the narrow, oddly flexible neck supporting it. Nacht can hold his head upright only by a constant effort of the will, and whenever he's thinking deeply about something, or falls into a state of absentmindedness, his head suddenly droops and his leaden chin hits his chest. To lift it back up he must gather all his strength, an effort that brings a florid bloom to his pale cheeks and imparts to his aged face those infantile features typical of the feebleminded.

Leopold Nacht—Poldy, as his closest friends call him—is an alcoholic. Like a diurnal ghost, his lanky figure haunts the downtown taverns from early dawn to dusk. But in spite of the etymology of his name, he is never seen in public at night: totally drunk, he stumbles off to sleep wherever he can.

Unlike most alcoholics, who, when they reach a certain level of intoxication, are prone to fall into a rage and begin rambling, Poldy remains grandly taciturn. When he enters one of his usual haunts and sees an acquaintance, he slowly directs his tottering steps towards him and *collapses* (literally) at his table. As a rule in such circumstances, his head suddenly rolls and freezes for a moment suspended upon his soft, unusually long neck. After drawing his head up, Poldy gazes at the other man with questioning, cloudy-blue eyes *but does not say a word*. His face remains impassive regardless of the response to this mute solicitation. If he gets a nod (obviously he never has money) Poldy emits a short, cavernous and disgusted command: Vodka! He drinks in silence; if someone addresses him, he answers with a simple, stock grimace or a mute gesture. It is a rare event to hear him utter a single word. When he does, it is only as a sign of particular respect for his interlocutor (for him, *language* seems to have a sacred character). After downing his glass of vodka, Poldy reassumes his interrogative gaze. Let us suppose that at this point his acquaintance has to leave, or is pressed for time, or out of money, or purely and simply, politely or brusquely, refuses him. Careful this time to hold his head erect, Poldy rises and departs, shuffling out in shoes covered with dust or mud, depending on the season. He never says goodbye, nor does he offer thanks.

In spite of appearances—which would justify the opinion that Leopold Nacht is a poverty-stricken degenerate with a mind darkened by alcoholism—Zacharias Lichter (in fact the only man with whom Poldy condescends to talk at greater length) considers him one of the great philosophers of contemporary Europe and, moreover, one of the very few that come near the experience of true *perplexity*. To enjoy Nacht's company, Zacharias Lichter often goes with Poldy on his pub rounds, although he himself never drinks, since his incandescent personality risks sudden and complete disintegration under the slightest ethylic assault.

"A blurry infinity of primordial waters rocks in Nacht's eyes"—Lichter was once telling a few friends in an excited tone of voice moved by rare reverence. "Those able to rise high enough to *comprehend* him see in the fractured, tense motion of his deformed hands—but oh how light, like the bones of a bird, of wings!—the gesture of a demiurge that brings forth burning comets to trace the dizzying depths of the spirit. His most trivial gestures—no matter how awkward or grotesque the practical world of stupidity may deem them—suspend all notion of weight. They are a breaking away, a tearing off, a painful disengagement from gravity. They are, at the same time, the initiation of an order where perplexity is Knowledge...

"God struck Nacht with the lightning bolt of purity; God *chose* him, maiming his body and giving him the cretinous countenance that he now bears with such *holiness*. In a corrupt world whose essence consists of degradation and decay, the fragility of the spiritual must be protected by ugliness, deformity, and disfigurement. Nacht has received the secret knowledge of self-protection through illness, through self-destruction. One by one, Nacht has lost almost all basic human instincts: hunger (like most alcoholics), the urge to reproduce, fear of death, and all social instincts in their various guises. This allows his sublime moments of collapse into perplexity, his aptitude to become a miniscule infinity within God and to encompass God within a greater infinity. This also engenders his exceptional aptitude for philosophy. His entire existence is a *meditation*, a meditation whose ultimate conclusion is *absolute muteness*, beyond speech or refusal of speech. Nacht's philosophy is a *philosophy of designification*: the world (inasmuch as it is a product of language) must be emptied of sense, and only then it will become one with Being. Being has no sense, it does not *signify*.

"Oh, how sick the world is with signifying! How I would like to learn from Nacht the art of remaining mute even while speaking (for the rare words he utters—a simple *con-*

*cession*, a concession I am the first to enjoy—never *mean* anything). I am there, I listen to him, I look at him, and his thinking, free of all signification, attracts me like a divine void. Oh, how I wish to become the *mute prophet* of the great Nacht! But will I ever rise to that height? Or am I doomed to remain forever what I have always been: a pitiful gabbler of abstractions."

... And Lichter's shining eyes darkened.

# FROM THE POEMS OF ZACHARIAS LICHTER

PSALM

God punished me for my innocence
(perhaps unwittingly I had been proud of it):
God covered me with mud and ashes,
for I was too clean,
He shattered my teeth and tore my tongue,
for I had praised him with words too sweet and beautiful
He maimed me,
for I was wending my way towards His land
with a stride too straight and strong.

God listened only to my mute prayers
showed me only what I could see without eyes,
sang to me only what I could hear without ears,
caressed me with a touch I could not feel,
filled my mouth with what I could not taste.
Blessed be the flame that is ravaging my being,
the flame that ignites my dry words,
the flame that ignites even my perishable shadow,
the flame of anguish and joy,
the terrible flame of God.

# ON WOMEN

"WHILE the eternal masculine consists essentially of what I would call the *genius of giving*"—Zacharias Lichter once explained to a young man who was parading misogynist opinions—"I identify the eternal feminine with the *genius of receptivity*. Only thus can I explain, for instance, this apparently curious fact: I experience a sense of being totally understood—a stimulating understanding that gives me wings and spurs me toward ever purer spaces—more often with women than men, even with the simplest of women. I have sometimes conversed for hours with a charwoman or some illiterate peasant selling her vegetables at market, and you know how forbidding and complicated my talk can be. Without making the slightest concession or condescending, hypocritically, to a more familiar and common level of language—and barring the initial reaction (startled confusion or stifled giggling)—I have always felt the joy of deeply fertile communication and found my spirit suffused with a rarely attained power.

"Undoubtedly, this complicity, this infectious communication, takes place on a metaverbal plane. Words no longer mean anything. They become bearers of an ineffable energy quite separate from any meaning: the presence of angels hovers above. Devoid of all semantic essence, words are mere vehicles of a reality beyond signifiers. Due to their extraordinary receptivity, women easily transcend typical masculine 'conventions'—the prejudice that communication can take place only within the codified limits of 'language.' They participate directly and intuitively in the essential flow of the spirit, in its fluxes and refluxes, which speech can sometimes *convey,* but never by *signifying.* Men who complain that women can't understand them, misogynists of all types, expect women to share their masculine conventions and stereotypes and to understand—with mechanical precision—their explicit language. In most cases, however, explicit language has no *living substance*; it is cold and dead."

# THE REVELATIONS OF
# BEGGING

BASED on his long experience as a beggar, Zacharias Lichter was able to analyze the inner structural tensions of those who gave him alms, even of those who gave nothing and passed by in total indifference, or tried to humiliate him with a scornful glance or dismissive word. He could do so in a fraction of a second, as if by a sudden illumination or flash of intellect, aided by a keen intuition equivalent in the moral order to sight in the spatial world. No one among those upon whom the prophet focused his piercing gaze (even had they realized what was happening and armed themselves against it) could have shielded even their most thickly veiled secrets from him.

At times, still under the impression of an unexpected discovery, or simply feeling the need to convey something he felt strongly about, whether positively or negatively, Zacharias Lichter would share with those nearest to him the observations, thoughts, and opinions formed during one or another of those humble days of begging. He would speak with emotion and respectful admiration about some passerby who had not even noticed him, or perhaps had only pretended not to, some stranger he had never seen before and would probably never see again. He would describe his particular characteristics in precise detail, as if he had spent years in close intimacy with him. At other times, conversely, he could not repress his violent revulsion at some lout who had insulted him in passing, or even someone who had given him alms.

"Nothing is more disgusting"—he would say—"than the charity of some beast with a human face, whose soul is filthier than a dirty nail. It's easy enough to see that particularly delicate natures may deny alms to a beggar out of embarrassment or shyness—both quite natural reactions. My experience, often bitterly painful, but infinitely precious for that very reason, has taught me that the act of *giving*, as well as its opposite, signifies absolutely nothing in itself.

"If some do not give, as I was saying, because they are reticent, out of an ineffable sense of delicacy (a delicacy fearful of the often overly brutal world of *seeming*), others refuse to give from a sense of pride and the false spirit of rigor that pride generates. Many don't give because they are in a hurry, or too lazy to make the effort, or simply short of change. (One cannot ask a beggar for cash back: only once, acting with the obvious cynicism of an aesthete, a fellow asked me to give him change. He had handed me a large banknote, accompanying his gesture with a questioning look as if facing a porter or a waiter; then, with an elegant and scornful gesture, he gave up. After all, his provocation, or more accurately, the *spectacle* of his provocation, had attained its goal, and had lent to *alms* the degrading sense of *baksheesh*, turning the beggar into a lowly *servant* by willfully and criminally degrading his spiritual prerogatives.) Some refuse to give out of inertia, others from miserliness, resentment, absentmindedness, or any of a thousand other reasons of which they prefer to remain unaware.

"Those who give are just as varied. Some give out of kindness, of course, but others, petty souls, do it merely to *demonstrate* to themselves how generous they are (a demonstration costing so little that the beggar, the poor beggar, often receives alms from the most tight-fisted of men). One person gives to show off in front of company, another from a vague superstition (a hope that the beggar's 'God bless you' might bring him *good fortune* through some sort of verbal magic).

"Just as some people don't give because they feel begging should not be allowed, others give almost exclusively out of an unconscious respect for the institution. Giving alms to a beggar may take on, for some, the significance of a participatory act, an empathetic gesture that enlarges the world's pool of *sympathy*. For others the same act means just the opposite, representing instead a proud, icy dissociation.

"Generally speaking"—Zacharias Lichter continued—"these days people pay little *attention* to begging itself or to their own practical attitude towards this ever-diminishing social category with all its paradoxes. Their level of attention has fallen so low as to be nearly nonexistent, and many give or don't give to beggars (the only beings to whom one can *give*) without even thinking. Some sudden urge may or may not impel them—and if asked, they would be hard-pressed to explain why. It is precisely this 'attenuation' of attention that provides the beggar, more than ever now, with a perspective that privileges moral observation. Knowing himself, he can gain a sudden yet deep insight into others. It is rare indeed that anyone reveals himself more clearly and unconsciously than before the outstretched hand of a wretched beggar on a street corner. The entire inner beauty or ugliness of the passerby may be concentrated in a simple look, an involuntary movement of the hand, the slightest frown, or some equally insignificant, casual gesture. Beneath the seemingly kind compassion of someone who drops a coin in the beggar's open hand, the keen-eyed recipient may suddenly discern, hideous and frightening, the cruel grimace of a monster, while barely a moment later he may be touched by a painful glow of candor and genuine courtesy hidden behind some banal, anonymous, and indifferent gaze.

"With this in mind, it's not too difficult to figure out why—especially for someone like me—the profession of begging is infinitely dangerous. Reacting to such violent shocks can be more debilitating than you'd think. Day after day I am obliged to witness what might be called 'a parade of monsters,' constantly interrupted—fortunately—by ineffable gleams of purity, yet inevitably recommencing beneath the same sign of dread, the same convulsion of the heart. For what could be, my God, more terrible than *seeing* the face of mercy among thousands of faces in which mercy is disfigured and soiled?

"Sometimes I receive alms from hands that seem to have moist tentacles or worms for fingers—I would throw the money away and spit with disgust were I not bound by one of the strictest and most inflexible laws of begging: accept everything, from everyone, with infinite humility… At other times, a slimy, imbecilic smirk pains and paralyzes me like venom spurting from a snake's fangs. Thereafter the image of Beauty itself leaves me inert, indifferent. When I beg"— Zacharias Lichter confessed—"I am prey to terrors and obsessions, to aversions and despair that no one would ever suspect. I don't know what would happen to me if the parade of monsters were not *constantly* interrupted by unseen yet blinding faces that shed a divine grace over the ugly world's ugliness. I owe my endurance, my strength to exist, repeatedly regained, to this constant alternation. It's true that for the most part I am unable to sense the effects, at once mysterious and manifest, of Mercy *at the time*. Only afterwards, in solitude, do I feel its dense illumination, its heavy, beneficial honey flowing into me."

# ON CHILDREN

WHEN THE weather is beautiful, Zacharias Lichter likes to take his lunch outdoors. His acquaintances know that he can be found around noontime in one of the parks or squares located in the city's center. After begging on one of the grand boulevards, Zacharias Lichter buys himself half a loaf of black bread and a jar of yogurt. He eats these slowly, on a bench, amongst nannies and old people, under the curious gaze of children of all ages who have come to play beneath the shade of the few melancholic and dusty trees growing in the heart of the city, amid asphalt and concrete.

Lichter's lunch seems to unfold according to some secret ritual: he takes from his pocket a small spoon wrapped in a scrap of newspaper, polishes it at length with the corner of his handkerchief, and examines its gleam for a while in the sunlight. Then he tears off a morsel of bread and holds the first bite in his mouth without chewing, as if in silent prayer. He does the same with the first spoonful of yogurt, holding it in his mouth until it dissolves completely. After a period in which he eats normally (although just as slowly), similar pauses follow, during which he is so withdrawn that if someone asks a question or addresses him, he not only does not answer but acts as if he hasn't heard a thing. Zacharias Lichter's behavior during his frugal meal is so strange that soon after he arrives, the bench on which he is seated is emptied, very discreetly, of other occupants. Although the regulars know him as a fellow who comes there on occasion to eat his yogurt and black bread in peace, the vague notion that he might be a madman makes them avoid him.

Children, however, have no such fear. In fact madmen seem to exert a special attraction for them. A few who happen to be about, and beyond their nannies' eyes, gather round Zacharias Lichter, who seems ready to talk with them and answer their most naive or impertinent questions. For him, childhood partakes of the eternal feminine: even boys, until they reach puberty (in spite of mimicking, often cartoonishly, "male" behavior), have feminine souls, hidden beneath an armor that is as much a warrior's as it is touchingly fragile. Like women, children also display the "genius of receptivity." Little by little and with exemplary patience Zacharias Lichter was able to make a few *friends* among them who were glad to listen to his long metaphysical monologues with a tense and grave attention, filled with almost religious respect.

"What draws me to children"—says Zacharias Lichter— "is their capacity to live naturally in the absurd and, conversely, to grasp the absurd aspects of the natural. Children have a vocation for paradise and only forcing them to adapt to social norms over time prevents them from following it. This is why God loves children. This is why His terrible and devastating flame softens as it touches them. The purity of children is one of the world's great mysteries. Children are pure not because they are 'good' (on the contrary, we know that many are quite cruel) or because they are 'innocent,' lacking an awareness of sin (which is a comfortable Jesuitical concept, since basic sins are almost always *unconscious*, and only minor ones at times involve free will), but perhaps because their spontaneous aptitude for life in paradise is stronger than the inertness of sin. This is, however, a mystery... In the great majority of cases maturity means the loss of a vocation for paradise. To lose paradise is to be expelled from childhood."

# ON POETRY

THE POET (while Zacharias Lichter is gazing at some distant point, rapidly blinking his swollen eyelids with their burnt lashes): What do you think of the verses I've just read to you?

ZACHARIAS LICHTER: They have a certain smooth sophistication and an awkwardness that may serve as a good path to the infinite. I can discern in those areas, but weakly, mind you, the rhythmic breathing of angels. Or, to put it in another way, I see large drunken butterflies slowly revolving in luminous dust. Your poems, at least some of them, undoubtedly have an incantatory power in which I hear an echo of the spiritual: an echo, however, coming from a very great distance. I think you've got too much talent...

THE POET: And you think talent is a liability?

ZACHARIAS LICHTER: In a way, yes. Because talent in poetry is simply *giving the impression that you are saying something* without actually saying anything. From this vantage point, poetry becomes just a preparation for *saying*, its aim is to create a focused attention in the ideal reader or listener, a state of receptivity towards a possible revelation, which, however, is never provided. This seems to me the very essence of the aesthetic: a game of preliminaries, the expectation, ever frustrated and ever renewed, of a revelation. *Homo aestheticus* (defined by the equation of *talent* with *taste*) delights in this incipience, where he can experience the voluptuousness of learned ambiguity, flirt verbally with silence, and make the means themselves—not without a tinge of "tragic" euphoria—seem their own end. The truth is that very few poets—only the great ones—manage to avoid this temptation: for talent is a temptation of the most dangerous kind.

THE POET: I find it impossible to counter your abstract accusations except by a "praise of poetry." Every poet worthy of the name invents *freedom*, thus affirming the infinite plasticity of the real in his own way: freedom which, in order to exist, must never resemble its own self. For the poet everything flows into everything else, the body becomes a flying tree, the star a stone, thought a trumpet of flames; grass turns blue and flows into the sky, the eyes are alpine lakes filled with God's tears. Ultimately, the poet swims through the universe as through an ever-changing sea of reflections.

ZACHARIAS LICHTER: Alas, this is so! Reflections flowing into reflections, words into words, games into games (without children). If only poetry were a reverse pedagogy that would teach us how to become children again! But no, the poetic game is one of cunning and deceit, imbued with death ... If poetry were at least—as it was for centuries—not an anticipation but a transcendence of *saying*, an opening beyond, an *ekstasis*—one of the means of ecstatic knowledge (as are all forms of love, no matter how humble). But no, poetry does not even say anymore. It pretends to say, it only pretends *to be* ...

And now let me confess something: I am afraid of poetry; I often feel that my religious vocation threatens to express itself only in the domain of religious poetry—which makes poetry itself seem a curse. After all—I wonder and shudder—am I myself anything other than a poet?

# RESPONSIBILITY AND FREEDOM

"AT EVERY moment"—Zacharias Lichter often repeats—
"I feel infinitely responsible for the fate of every individual
included—alas, here too I bear responsibility—in the old,
corrupt word *humanity*. From the most savage crime to the
fleeting smile of sadness on the lips of a child, nothing happens in the world for which I am not responsible, for which
I have not taken on—openly, before God, seized by shame,
fear, and disgust—responsibility.

"I am contemporary with our entire history: I am guilty
of all the wars that have bloodied the earth; I am the one
who ordered all massacres, who carried out all injustices. I
am, repeatedly, by virtue of the huge palingenetic force of
evil, the torturer, the inquisitor, the signatory of all death
sentences: death by decapitation, death by hanging, im-
molation, and on the wheel, death by flaying, drowning,
poisoning, death by starvation. I am the inventor of all
psychological torture, the harvester of suspicion, the analytic
organizer of all obsessions and terrors, collective and individual. I am all these and many more. I, Zacharias Lichter;
I, the prophet-clown; I, the beggar...

"I know my guilt, I proclaim it and wish to be punished;
but the certitude that no one will ever punish me, that I will
be denied the sweet pain of retribution for all eternity, weighs
heavily upon me.

"*Hell is the absence of punishment*, the yearning for chastisement; and responsibility is the hell of conscience. I have no right to choose; I myself have been *chosen*—God *chose* me—to answer for all the mistakes, past, present, and future, of my fellow creatures.

"My freedom is a paradox, an *irony*, a paroxysmal form of irony, a question open to any answer. So then, I feel *bound* to answer: it's *me*.

"Ah! Even forgiveness would be a punishment. But who will forgive me? I am denied even the right to punish myself. I have no right other than to accuse myself to the very end, without any consequences.

"Yes, I am the one guilty of all crimes, rapes, incest; I unleashed all misfortunes, caused all misdeeds, trampled on all laws. I, Zacharias Lichter."

# ON ONE FORM OF DIVINE
# WRATH

BESIDES Leopold Nacht, and certainly not on equal foot-
ing with him, we count among Zacharias Lichter's friends
one of the most picturesque exemplars of the fauna that
populates the city's taverns. At first sight, no link, even accidental, seems possible between Lichter and this man, who
displays all the features of an aggressive thug mired in the
attitudes of slum violence, a walking incarnation of resentment and low-life promiscuity. A drunk, ever ready for scandal or a scuffle, glib with slang, spewing endless obscenities
(he speaks fast, words pouring from his lips in short bursts,
with intermittent pauses during which he turns his head to
spit a thin jet of saliva through his green teeth), slovenly
dressed and filthy, with the air of a man who sleeps under
bridges at night, giving off the smell of the canal, yet in spite
of all, pleasant to look at, with a strong, well-proportioned
body and an incredible smile that lights up his face—he is
known in the world of taverns by the sobriquet *the Poet*.

And indeed he writes verses, generally of a pornographic
nature, which he recites drunkenly, in a falsely pathetic tone,
like sweet, soulful ballads, to anyone who will listen. Of
course people laugh (his favorite dish, a hymn of praise to
the phallus, does not lack a certain strength, grandeur, and
obvious talent, a rough talent for brutal spontaneity, which

Zacharias Lichter metaphorically describes as a "superb Fury smashing the boudoir mirrors of self-indulgence").

A curious fact in the relationship between Zacharias Lichter and the Poet-Thug is that the latter sympathizes and is even fond, in his way, of the prophet, yet shows no respect for his ideas. On the contrary, he subjects them to unwarranted and trivial jokes, which he spews forth with frenetic glee. Yet Zacharias Lichter continues telling him about God's flame and the abysses of perplexity with true fervor, as if speaking to someone receptive to his words, or at least potentially so: glowing and radiant, he patiently explains the principles of the Dialectics of Purity and the Discipline of Ecstatics. Then he listens with gentle surprise and even—curiously—an air of acquiescence, to the other's replies, which are drowned in roars of laughter. Asked once by some young disciples how he accounted for such passivity, Zacharias Lichter replied:

"From God's point of view, vulgarity does not exist, so there is no reason to be shocked. The hyperbolic delirium of the slum, which casts its garbage in the face of the stupid, bespattering their cotton-wool souls with its slops, spreading its stench over the dainty fainting spells of well-bred prostitutes—this delirium is imbued with the *essence of divine wrath*.

"I might say"—Lichter went on—"that I delight in the cruel mockery, in the pestilential climate into which my words and ideas are dragged. At such moments I feel a highly spiritual voluptuousness ... Angels sometimes like to soar among cracked and dirty mirrors glazed by greenish vapors, fly-specked, and soiled by the grease of narrow brows that once pressed against them. Without knowing it, this hoodlum, brawling and obscene, prepared to spit on anything, is closer to the metaphysical condition than some subtle intellectual whose high-pitched arguments justify outworn commonplaces long defunct and therefore particularly comfortable ... In his vast and confused revolt, he unknowingly delivers a divine message. His feet soil the downy pillows on which the complacent sleep, his fists shatter the windows of the brothels of *decency*, his words dynamite the inert calm of all prejudice. He is the annihilator of myths."

# ON TRAVEL

FOR YEARS now, since the moment he first discovered his spiritual calling, Zacharias Lichter has not left the city. He is indifferent to the beauties of nature; what attracts him to city parks is the peace and quiet cherished by urban dwellers sick of the mechanical rumblings of modern life. Zacharias Lichter visited the seaside a few times as a student, during vacations, but the scorching sun, the salt-laden wind from the open sea, heavy with the odor of algae and rotting shells, the entire climate of the beach, produced in him such a state of organic imbalance mixed with an unpleasant giddiness that he gave up. At about that same time he took his only trip to the mountains but returned, prey to a strange anxiety, after a few hours in an alpine railway station. The rocky cliffs of the riverbed along which the railroad serenely wound its way seemed to him of such dizzying heights that they might topple at any moment. He feared the first whistle of the locomotive would release a catastrophic avalanche. At the station where he got off and spent a few hours waiting for the return train, the distant shouts coming now and then from the mountain filled him with terror. But beyond these innocent idiosyncrasies, Zacharias Lichter also came to condemn the modern taste for travel from the elevated perspective of his prophetic mission.

"The pleasure of travel"—Lichter says—"is one of the

most pernicious forms of self-indulgence. The universal dissolves to the picturesque, the essential crumbles to the accidental and kaleidoscopic. The revelations that the leisurely traveler pretends to experience do not go beyond the low order of *surprise*.

"In our epoch, with rare exceptions, travel has become a subjective need, a desire that, if unsatisfied, drives some people into pathetic states of self-delusion—a desire to live in the sweet deception of appearances, in soothing availability. Undoubtedly, the modern traveler's entire psychology is ruled by *availability* and *lack of responsibility*, converted into an effervescent eagerness, the excited tipsiness of *curiosity*. The tourist keeps turning the world into a variety show meant to provide for and stimulate his digestion—on a moral plane. For indeed his spirit functions in perfect analogy to a digestive system that feeds on *impressions*. We should not be at all surprised that in the grand and ever-growing Realm of Stupidity, the taste for travel is highly evolved. Periodically, all practical and sustained effort needs a relaxing dose of tourism and entertainment to stimulate and enhance the 'joy of work.'

"The true nature of pleasure is to aspire to intensities capable of annihilating pleasure itself at any moment. I cannot imagine great gluttons other than as padded in thick layers of fat, elevating the pleasure of taste until it reaches an altitude of anguish. I envision striking exemplars of sloth increasing their passivity to a point of such ambiguity that it begins to resemble asceticism, metaphorically attaining a purely vegetative state. True, the pleasure of idiots involves much more ordinary modes, taking the form of the minor thrills of tourism and other vague and illusory satisfactions, subject to availability."

# FROM THE POEMS OF ZACHARIAS LICHTER

## MOUTH FULL OF FLOWERS

Beggars, lunatics, old friends,
It's been raining so long and we have no shelter,
It rains of winter, of spring, and of other seasons,
It rains of thought and of death, and without purpose, it
    rains
Of fright and of cold words, of words, words,
Beggars, lunatics, putrid nights
Illuminated solely by the eyes of the wandering Prophet,
Nights of wet ash and dimmed signs,
And of drowned things, oh, of long wakes,
Years of water, hours of wind, unending Sundays (words
Cold, ancient, troubled, laden with fate),
Nights of fierce rain, with beggars and lunatics,
Friends traversing the desert of memories
Mouth full of flowers.

# THE CRIME OF "ANALYSIS"

THE ACQUISITION of authentic knowledge always ends in paradox and mystery. Only those mired in the presumption of the *known* can possibly believe that in the realm of authenticity and thus that of the spiritual, to know is to analyze, for to analyze means to destroy. Zacharias Lichter never tires of repeating: "The desire to analyze someone, anyone at all, is a wish to kill that person. In the moral order, the analyst is a vampire, a genius of crime."

The vampirism of analysis is embodied, Zacharias Lichter believes, in a certain man of dull appearance, correctly dressed, and sober in demeanor, who enjoys a solid reputation as a psychiatrist: we are talking about Doctor S., in whose presence Lichter is overcome by nervousness and even fear, which he is of course at pains to conceal. As a consequence, although Doctor S. shows an interest in all that Lichter says and does, and makes every effort to demonstrate his sympathy and even friendship (which given the doctor's social standing would flatter anyone), Lichter systematically avoids him. If the unavoidable happens and the two find themselves face to face, Zacharias Lichter loses his composure, is brushed by the soft wing of timidity, stammers when he has to reply to a question, and withdraws into long periods of disoriented silence . . .

"I feel his analytical mind stalking me aggressively"— Lichter confesses to those close to him—"I can feel it preparing to fascinate me, to paralyze me. Doctor S. is not interested (although he pretends to be) in *knowing* me (the act of knowing presupposes an infinitely discreet communication in mystery) but wants instead, with incredible cruelty, to *define* me, to ensnare me in the rigid geometrical traps of his definitions, to catch me in the poisonous spiderwebs of the known. He wants to commit moral assassination … And he shows no concern that I have thus far eluded him. To the genius of crime he adds the genius of patience.

"I must admit that of all the people I've been fated to encounter, Doctor S. alone arouses in me an almost pathological fear. It is sheer fright, with no physical component. It is the spirit afraid to plunge into a mirage, yet unable to escape, frozen in the clear and rigid ice of that mirage, eternally, like the damned in the last circle of Dante's *Inferno*. Using his vast and lifeless science, slowly and methodically, Doctor S. has started to construct an image of me that is absolutely *false* yet at the same time *refined* and *subtle*; an image that, once completed (I hope this will never happen), threatens to absorb me in the perfection of its unreality.

"The mechanism of his stupidity—you will have guessed that Doctor S. is one of the most illustrious citizens of the Realm of Stupidity—functions with such amazing precision, so flawlessly, that I am hard put not to feel a kind of terrified admiration for him. I am convinced that if he managed to define me (and I avoid him to keep that from happening), my sublime spiritual madness, detached from all that is *objectively mysterious* in it, would suddenly become in effect some rare type of mystical mania. And my entire spiritual adventure—diminished to an 'interesting case'—would end with my deplorable but seemingly just incarceration in a lunatic asylum.

"Many are guilty of the crime of analysis (or at least of its intent, since most people lack the means to carry it out). All that is indecipherable, unique and mysterious in a human being, all that pertains to the essence of the great existential paradoxes, has become the target of a hidden aggression, of a glacial ferocity consisting of analysis and reduction to the already known: tools made more efficient by the greater abundance of the elements of the known, allowing for a larger number of possible combinations. Thus the case of Doctor S., whose extremely penetrating stupidity represents for me—and clearly not just for me alone—a perpetual threat and a mortal danger."

# ON SUICIDE

To a young man who once confessed he harbored thoughts of suicide, Zacharias Lichter explained: "Some think—or, even more strongly—are convinced that freedom is possible only as *refusal* or *negation*. Consequently, *suicide* appears to them as the supreme manifestation of individual freedom, the only voluntary means of extricating oneself from all determinism. From that vantage point, suicide acquires a clear theoretical seductiveness and becomes a *philosophical problem*.

"Let us not deceive ourselves: the actual act of self-negation is not the result of a thought process that ends in a value judgment ('life is not worth living'). On the contrary, the decision to commit such an act seeks to find a wider justification and to define itself as an attribute of the 'human condition.' In the final analysis, the suicide's despair (regardless of its theoretical clothing) remains an individual case, a paroxysmal form of psychological resentment. After all, no one commits suicide because life is absurd, but only because, consciously or unconsciously, life does not appear absurd enough. The suicide believes that his act increases the absurdity of existence. Committing suicide is therefore not a way of refusing life (as it may seem) but the ultimate expression of resentment on the part of those who think life is refusing them. Life appears beautiful to them, and because this beauty seems inaccessible, they wish to soil it. Life seems to make sense and they wish (a vain and childish hope) to render it absurd . . .

"We must recognize, however, that the resentment of a potential suicide (no matter how detestable in itself, as any resentment is) must be classified as tragic, since it derives from an *error*: that of endowing existence with marvelous attributes, of construing it as a sort of terrestrial paradise from which they are excluded and thus wish to destroy. The lack of any religious dimension in their life renders them incapable of discerning life's fundamental absurdity. Truly, no one who has attained a genuine and deep awareness of the absurdity of existence would commit suicide: the act would be pointless and, on a deeper level, utterly irresponsible. Is it conceivable that Job would have dared to consider, even for an instant, such a solution?

"Leaving aside the deeper meaning it implies, the act of suicide also reveals something of its essence in its more common psychological attributes. We all know, for example, that the threat of suicide is often used as emotional blackmail in romantic 'dramas.' Even supposing that a person may shorten his life for purely theoretical reasons (which are in reality mere 'sublimations' of more concrete, if more obscure, reasons), suicide still retains an element of blackmail: it wants to be the final cue of a dialogue, the fulfillment of a promised revenge.

"To the extent that it is an act of vengeance (the vengeance of impotence), suicide aspires to elevate itself to *tragic spectacle*. Suicides rarely attempt to make the act appear an accident. They want it to be known, to arouse obsessions, to engender irreparable regret, to create in an individual or even a community (as in the case of political suicides) a guilty conscience. Even suicides that seem *noble* when viewed from afar tend covertly to cast an ugly light on life, to embitter, to rend or sully some aspect of life.

"I exclude here, of course, suicide as sacrifice, extremely rare in our times, which can be one of the sublime forms of martyrdom; I also exclude suicide committed by the frightened prisoner who knows he will be tortured, or those condemned to death, or the incurably ill who can no longer stand the pain—these are equally rare because, in most cases, such people lack the means to carry out their intentions. As a matter of fact, in all these cases suicide is no longer a truly *free act*, it loses all polemical meaning and in any case makes no statement of any kind. In its ultimate humility, it is the equivalent of a simple, ordinary death.

"In all other cases, suicides—incapable of recognizing the absurdity of existence—are estranged from God by the arrogance that masks their hatred of life. Most believe that their gesture will ennoble them. Insofar as they consider themselves aristocrats of the tragic, believing their entire existence will acquire a higher meaning in retrospect, seeing themselves crowned with the halo of myth, these aspirants to suicide illustrate—no matter how surprising this seems— one aspect of *self-indulgence*. But then, who doesn't flirt with the idea of suicide; who doesn't clothe it in all sorts of grotesquely sentimental guises in order to console their souls; who does not sometimes seek a small welcoming oasis of gratification in the midst of life's vicissitudes? For these worms of the earth, suicide is one of the easiest forms in which self-indulgence manifests itself, one of the most odious means of 'compensation.' But come to think of it, in the great majority of cases, not even actual suicides manage to escape a touch of self-indulgence . . .

"And now"—Lichter ended his monologue with a sudden surge of anger—"now that you know what I think about suicide, and since you'll never understand the Word that burns my tongue and rends my lips, that disfigures my face, go hang yourself, or may I never see you again!"

# ON COMFORT

ZACHARIAS Lichter discovered long ago that people who share the cult of *comfort* (combined with that of "utility") fear any manifestation of the spiritual, no matter how timid and unassuming, as if it were some obscure, and thus even more dangerous, disease. Any unexpected emotional reaction (no matter how insignificant), any surprising thought or desire, especially one that may seem to involve (however wrongly) a spiritual dimension, creates anxiety and concerns that do not cease until these moments are *defined*, explained, and diagnosed—that is, wrenched from the unknown. The comfort of stupidity presupposes a strict prophylaxis with regard to the spiritual...

Adrian Leonescu, a young professor of English phonetics, seems expressly created to exemplify, almost in caricature, the basic mechanisms of comfort. In spite of his leonine name, he displays all the characteristics of the effete: a thin voice that, with effort, can be lowered to mezzo-soprano, a smooth white skin covered in fine down, languorous eyes, narrow shoulders, and wide hips that swing just so when he walks. His only masculine attribute, contrasting with his entire countenance, is a rough black beard, which he shaves twice a day, morning and afternoon, with the scrupulous attention of those hirsute women who depilate themselves.

Leonescu was barely a teenager when he found his minor

vocation, which he has since pursued with rigorous tenacity: English phonetics, which he seems to consider a cult of purely verbal sonority. He has assimilated English with thorough diligence, memorizing textbooks and even entire dictionaries by rote. His greatest pride is his matchless *pronunciation* of English in all its variations: from London cockney to pure Oxonian, from Yorkshire dialect to American drawl, each with the nuances of regional, social, and ethnic strata. Since words themselves hold no interest for him, engrossed as he is solely in their phonetic qualities, he practices these exercises with a shameless sensual voluptuousness, resorting exclusively and almost affectedly to clichés and common phrases.

Adrian Leonescu's complete lack of interest in ideas is compensated for by his remarkable ability to pronounce words. His entire physical and moral being participates in what is an almost mystical act: when he starts to produce English phrases, his languorous eyes suddenly turn sightless, his features become so tense that even if the words are comical, he is unable to even sketch a smile, the veins on his brow swell and pulse. If he is walking, his legs grow heavy, as if weighed down by a ball and chain; his elbows are clamped to his sides and his fingers clutch stiffly at the lapels of his coat. Only his fleshy lips, standing out redly against a livid face fixed in concentration, are mobile and elastic. From deep within, as if emerging from a great distance, a thin and tremulous but always correct verbal stream gushes forth.

Adrian Leonescu leads a hygienic existence, both mental and corporeal: *mens sana in corpore sano*. The old adage is put into practice, among other things, thanks to his slight case of "preventive hypochondria," which makes him exaggerate vague symptoms and even invent a few. He then subjects himself to medical treatments which—and this shows his extreme prudence—cannot possibly harm him. His hypochondria is never more than a defense mechanism, and this applies as well to his medication, which he never abuses. The truth is that Adrian Leonescu takes loving care of his health. He exercises every morning with the windows to his room wide open and keeps at his disposal—a true claim to glory—a complicated rowing machine. He takes daily walks and, in order not to waste time, always carries along a dictionary, diligently and patiently memorizing arcane meanings or unusual pronunciations. As a phonetician, his voice clearly receives special attention: like an opera singer, Adrian Leonescu rinses his mouth with raw eggs, neither smokes nor drinks, and performs lip exercises in front of the mirror. A reputable doctor provides him with optimal dietary regimens, modifying them if he complains of slight dyspepsia or a bout of constipation, or shows vague signs of cholecystitis, spastic colitis, splenomegaly, or the like. A sexologist has prescribed an erotic regimen: once or, at most, twice a week and, if possible, with the same woman (which has led the poor man to enter into an unhappy marriage).

Adrian Leonescu's greatest worry is his nervous system. He is beset by obscure anxieties, which he combats with modest doses of sedatives; nevertheless they continue to reoccur—admittedly not in any serious form—with a kind of stubborn persistence. Like all who live with comfort in mind, Adrian Leonescu is worried because he worries.

At one point, these recurring anxieties managed to produce a state of true alarm. At a gathering where Zacharias Lichter found himself by chance, Adrian Leonescu once confessed, in dramatic tones of voice:

"I've been feeling awful lately. My anxieties, which I've never come to terms with, seem to have multiplied, and I can't explain why. To top it all off, a few nights ago I woke around one a.m. and, out of the blue, my eyes filled with tears and I felt like praying to God, God forbid! I was so scared I stayed up all night. The next day I went to the doctor and—this made me feel even worse—he looked astonished, although he then tried to calm me down. Can you imagine what a nuisance all this is? Apparently, it's a standard neurasthenic depressive syndrome. The doctor prescribed mental rest, so tomorrow I leave for the mountains..."

"It's incredible"—Lichter burst out after the phonetician's departure—"what grotesque and abject forms an imbecile's fear can take on when confronted by the inexplicable and mysterious. In a way it's quite natural for this to happen. Any weakness or negligence in that area, no matter how small, may release massive landslides in which the edifice of stupidity could be buried forever. Just as those capable of genuine spiritual life are wary of being defined and thus deprived of the profound absurdity of their own existence, fools fear they might be 'uncovered,' might lose the protection of the *known* when faced with the threat of the mysterious, which, in their eyes, takes on the import of a malefic and monstrous force. The comfort of fools does not deny— why bother?—the existence of a nominal and conventional God, a God that guarantees a degree of discipline and even mental hygiene necessary for foolishness to function. But comfort sees the slightest shadow of true spirituality as the sign of a disturbing illness that must be *diagnosed* at once and firmly treated. You can be cured of God by sedatives and sleeping pills, by Swedish gymnastics and trips to the mountains—how awful it is! In the Realm of Stupidity, comfort is the primary precondition for any activity. Comfort is also its value and ultimate goal: no effort is too great for fools when it comes to being comfortably settled in. In point of fact, they never *act*, they *settle in*, regardless of the activity, their constant concern is to let nothing trouble them."

# ON MATHEMATICAL LANGUAGE

SHORT and rotund, yet moving with incredible briskness, casting small gestures in all directions that suggest not only inexhaustible energy but also a sort of curious, unfocused *dexterity*; with lively, rolling eyes that enhance the already unusual mobility of his entire physiognomy (a mobility that has nothing to do with anxiety or concern)—thus does the mathematician W. present himself to us. This scholar of some repute is also one of our city's most picturesque figures, one you would swear must be wearing his legs off, so tirelessly does he stride through its streets from morn till evening. You would not be surprised, then, to see him turn up wherever you happen to be, rolling along towards you with improbable speed, with the express aim of stopping you (even if he only knows you slightly) and making you listen to him.

His physical vivacity (surprising in someone so corpulent) is matched by an equally remarkable mental vivacity that expresses itself in a voluble, unrestrained, almost crazed verbal stream. Although he speaks in a hasty tone and rhythm akin to mere *chatter*, the mathematician W. never strays from the rigorous field of his preoccupations, to which he imparts an air (perfectly false, however) of accessibility. An occasional—and it's seldom more than occasional—interlocutor feels attracted by his speculations. No matter how abstruse and inextricably complex his thoughts, he pours them forth with gusto and forcefulness, with a talent for creating a sense of humorous complicity normally restricted to those who tell jokes well. But W. "tells" only pure abstractions.

As a child he had already distinguished himself by his extraordinary precocity. Even now (he has been recently promoted to associate professor), the renown he enjoys is based in large part on his contributions at the age of twelve to number theory. His more recent work, primarily in topology, has not enjoyed a similar reception. In that field he discovered, some time ago, a fundamental theorem whose proof took him eight long years to complete. Unfortunately—slanderous tongues assure us—to follow his proof step by step would require as much time and exertion as that expended by its author. No one has wished to take on such task (and truth be told, no one has even tried)—so that this major theorem, neither contested nor accepted, remains fodder for petty and malicious gossip, and not only in specialist circles.

Faced with a situation that would have tested anyone's patience and peace of mind, the mathematician W. remained completely serene. "Future decades"—he would say—"will prove me right, since it is clear that even if the theorem is wrong (and I've never claimed otherwise), it is extremely *fertile*. In fact, I must confess that I've already found a few errors in my proof. One can *demonstrate*, however (and I am undertaking this now), that these are errors of genius: each could bring forth a wholly new branch of topology. After all"—he would ask rhetorically—"isn't the entire history of the so-called exact sciences a history of errors endowed with a high coefficient of fertility?" (The paradoxical spirit of mathematician W. defines *truth* as a totally sterile error.)

An open and sociable character par excellence, W. is, as we have seen, ready to talk to anyone, anytime and anywhere:

in a waiting room, in a crowded tram, on a street corner, and even, if invited, in some dive. Not to mention pastry shops, the true temples of his gustatory delight, where he freely places himself at the mercy of extreme pleasure while consuming sweets—the only excess he allows himself. (He indeed has an insatiable hunger for anything sweet, from the candy that always fills his pockets to rich cakes with thick layers of cream he can hardly wait to eat, swallowing them whole, smearing his face like a child.) He does not discriminate among those willing to listen to him; he may be encountered in motley bohemian gatherings as well as pretentious intellectual circles.

As a rule, very few people have any idea what his theories are about, but that doesn't prevent most people from being overcome, in his presence, by a strange euphoria, a type of purely mental intoxication, a sense of being lifted upward, of smooth ascension towards the firmament of numbers. Almost all commend the mathematician's great intelligence and especially his force of persuasion (which never convinced anybody of anything except its own existence). In fact, directly or indirectly, W. has been offering an unending eulogy of the mathematical spirit, and it is very probable that, over time, he has come to regard himself not only as its representative, but as its vessel or incarnation. This, at least, is how Zacharias Lichter, who had the opportunity to converse with him on a number of occasions, perceived him.

"Thanks to this man"—he said—"I've come to realize one of the essential features of the mathematical spirit, namely, its narcissism. It is obvious that mathematical language neither desires nor is able to express anything but itself. It is a language that turns its back to the *real* and, preoccupied exclusively with its immanent precision, contemplates itself as pure language, born of pure conventionality. In the field of mathematics, truth and falsehood cease to be regarded as values: the simple fact that a theorem is false does not mean anything to the mathematician, since the very *consciousness of falsehood* can lead to the discovery of new exactitudes and new means by which mathematical language explores its own self. Innocent at first sight, mathematical narcissism reveals its wickedness when its spirit *is transposed into practice*. Putting mathematical knowledge into practice (which the ancient Greeks avoided, intuiting its dangers) is by no means a confirmation of its truth value in an ontological sense. It is nothing more than the possibility of transferring language and linguistic devices from the ideal plane onto the material one. This is shown, among others, by all modern technology, which could be considered a mode of reproducing or simulating, mechanically, the operations of mathematical language. For centuries on end, tools were perceived (starting from an *organic* model) as extensions of the human hand; today, the typical tools of civilization appear clearly as extensions of mathematical language. The world in which we live tends to place itself, without our even realizing it, under the sign of *tautology*, under the sign of Narcissus turned mathematician. Its symbol could be (and actually is) this restless little man, whose mind does nothing else but invent *games*, games that play, endlessly, with their own inventions. Beyond his explicit statements, he keeps repeating one and the same thing: *Truth is dead!* And this claim, which should make us shudder, does not bother us in the least."

# A POEM TOSSED INTO THE TRASH BIN OF A PUBLIC GARDEN BY ZACHARIAS LICHTER AND RETRIEVED BY HIS BIOGRAPHER

How distant is nearness
how distinct darkness
how simple is intricacy
how intricate simplicity
divinely large the small
divinely meek the grand
divinely clear the vague as well
and sharp as ice the disgust
and luminously great the thirst
by thirst itself pervaded
and darkly vast the tidings
the old word-rag in the mouth
the word that tells nothing
a world submerged in fog
that the tongue thrusts through
how it tastes of fog in silence
how distant is nearness

# ON OLD PEOPLE

"OLD PEOPLE"—Zacharias Lichter was once saying—"are on intimate terms with both life and death . . . Their possessions diminish (together with their aptitude for possession) and sometimes disappear, melting away like vapor into the air. Little by little old age *impoverishes* them. Even if some still seem wealthy, they all face the pure, naked, and ineffable obliteration of being.

"Obviously, I'm not thinking of active, energetic, *well-preserved* old people, whose age, though advanced, is still abstract and somehow theoretical. Those can be, and often are, true monsters of resentment and hate. (Classical characterology teaches us that we can winnow from among them the *misers*; and also some of the cruelest agents of power: inflexible tormentors, inquisitors and gray eminences who lurk in shadows, and many others, petty and insignificant, who turn, violently and cold-heartedly, against those closest to them or even against themselves.) Not of those am I thinking, but of the ones with bodies broken by the years; apoplectics with impotence deeply embedded in their flesh; decrepit beings with foggy minds and tear-filled eyes brimming with infinite kindness and placid stupor; the weak and the deaf, stammering with soft, viscous speech, forgetting everything a moment later, crippled by every affliction of old age, parading shy and imbecilic smiles; those who, drained by years of sleep deprivation, can no longer fall asleep or even dare to hope to—their life swathed in *murkiness*, sanctified by the lack of all desire, ashamed even at the thought that they might still desire, unless the very memory of desire itself has left them ...

"Of these grand old people I am thinking, those crushed by the world's weariness; of the shallow fountain of their conscience, so clear that invisible angels are mirrored in it."

A while back an old woman passed away in a narrow and damp shack located in the courtyard facing Zacharias Lichter's crumbling garage. She was of such advanced age that she could no longer keep track of her years, nor did her relatives, who had abandoned her in the hope that neglect would hasten her demise. She had shrunk, curled over, and could barely drag herself along in a world crammed with shadows and strange, muffled, unreal sounds, heard as if from afar. Sleep had long since deserted her: she was spending her nights lying on her fir-wood bed and straw mattress, often mumbling indistinctly with her eyes open. It was perhaps her way of *dreaming*, of relieving herself of the unknown burdens that dreams usually disperse. Frail as a bird, helpless, she would have dwindled away sooner—to the satisfaction of her relatives, who for all that must have felt some remorse—had she not been cared for by a few good-hearted neighbors, and especially by Zacharias Lichter, who owed her a debt of gratitude. For it was she who had presented him with the Bible.

Her sight was so weakened that, no longer able to discern letters, she had asked him to read to her from the holy book whenever he had the time. And this Lichter did, accompanying his reading with passionate comments, really quite unsuitable for the pious, simpleminded crone's trivially superstitious comprehension. But this did not matter in the least. Even less so as shortly afterwards the old woman also lost her hearing: she knew she was being read to but was unable to distinguish any words in that distant flow. Even so, perhaps more than ever, she was happy someone was talking to her—even if more and more hazily, more dimly and more vaguely; and just as on other occasions, Lichter immersed himself totally in what he was saying, with that expansive passion and persuasive force which, while not moving the other, kept seeking out new, mysterious, and inexhaustible resources.

Other than that, the old woman got by on almost nothing. When it came to food, she ate like a sparrow; a mug of water, brought by someone from the pump in the yard, sufficed her for an entire day. A few drops quenched her thirst and the rest she used to wash herself as best she could, poor soul, in the rusty basin she kept in her tiny room with its warped walls. Every other day, Lichter or someone else would sweep the floor and tidy up her things. Those who entered were struck by the simplicity and cleanliness of the interior (in spite of the pungent, apparently sourceless odor of mold; for mold is not a sign of filth but of the abandoned, the outmoded, of oblivion, its odor almost abstract). The old woman usually sat all day long in a chair. In winter it was drawn up near the cast-iron stove on which a tin plate filled with sand had been placed to keep the room warm; from spring to fall, in fine weather, she sat outside the low door in the heat of the sun. She sat quietly, without seeming to expect or want anything. Her eyes stared ahead blankly, with the tinge of a lifeless smile imprinted on her furrowed visage, whose dry wrinkles, when seen up close, recalled geological strata frozen in time.

Her hours appeared to pass in unperturbed, mysterious, unspoken joy. It was hard to say if she recognized anyone (who knows, though, perhaps in the wraith-like beings who approached her and now and then addressed her in garbled words, she may have recognized dear old faces, because tears would sometimes come to her eyes). It was equally hard to decide if she knew who she was anymore—she may well have forgotten her own name, for she had long since ceased to use it, and those who cared for her in her old age never did: they called her *Măicuță* or "Little Mother" (some, I think, still recalled her name, but Lichter, at any rate, never knew it).

"What use is it to live in such a state of imbecility"—someone said, interrupting Zacharias Lichter's poignant discourse on the meaning of old age just at the point where he was evoking his rapport with the poor old woman, who had recently passed away—"when you're no longer of use to anyone and have no idea what a burden you are to others or the predicament you pose? What sense is there in a life like that?"

"What use? What sense?"—Zacharias Lichter flared up—"... never have I felt more deeply imbued with pure existence than when I faced that woman. God, how much I learned from her nearly sightless eyes. Old people, and old people alone, can teach us, in our ignorance—without words, beyond words—what it means *to be*. Only they can unveil, if only for a moment, the divine miracle of *being*, that being we all experience unconsciously in childhood and which we may never experience again. In itself, in its mysterious essence, *old age is a blessing*.

"A blessing bearing the wisdom of existence, lifted not only beyond possessions—in the ordinary sense of the word— but also beyond our inner possessions, the accumulations of our personal memories, our own past (because we *have* our past, because what we were turns into having, into a paradoxical possession, whose present nonbeing we cherish so dearly)...Old age is Rising just as birth is Falling. Rising and shedding all that clung to our being as it rolled in the dirt of the world: so many endless false entanglements. Extreme old age is a natural and universal catharsis, a purification...

"How rare true old age is, however! How fiercely we fight against its wisdom! And thus, instead of standing speechless with awe and love in its presence, instead of worshiping it on our knees, we even ask ourselves: 'What use is it to live in such a state of imbecility?' No use, of course, not the slightest: for wisdom is beyond use, useless in its pure silence! What sense could it have? Of course, no sense whatever: for old age truly begins where all sense ends, where nothing *has* significance, where everything *is*...Pure transcendence and pure overflowing into the nothingness of language. The sacred power of making the word face its void, of filling it with that void.

"Talking to that old woman, to *Măicuţă*"—Zacharias Lichter was saying—"I felt that *my mission was being fulfilled*: as if I had talked to a child or to Leopold Nacht...But no, Leopold Nacht humbles me with his silence, makes me feel ashamed of my need to talk. My 'Little Mother,' on the other hand, gave me the feeling that talking is not totally a curse, that a gleam of holiness can spring from language and that language can find its deeper meaning in its very lack of significance..."

# ON SAYING AND WRITING

ZACHARIAS Lichter wrote rarely: a poem he'd been carrying about in his head for a long time or a stray, stubborn thought that threatened to become a poem. Perhaps he wrote to "free" himself, to dispel those words that, against his will, kept repeating themselves obsessively in identical, nagging succession. Writing for him was not so much an act of expression as a desire to sweep away some prior, overly crystallized form of expression, to dissolve and wash it from his memory in order to return to what, in Lichterian terms, one might call *creative forgetting*.

Jotted down hastily in an irregular, almost illegible hand on the margin of a newspaper or some scrap of paper picked up who knows where, Zacharias Lichter's poems or poetic fragments were usually thrown away instantly or abandoned on the very spot where they were created. This habit, aided by happenstance, enabled his biographer to come into possession of a few. Clearly their author cared nothing for them, and one supposes (at least one familiar with his way of thinking) that the simple act of writing them down filled Lichter with unavowed *shame*. To go so far as to gather and keep them, to assume their paternity, would have been in his eyes the epitome of self-abasement. And so indeed it would have been, had not the prophet—as we know him—serenely ignored even the possibility of doing so.

"The fiery truth"—Zacharias Lichter would say—"can only be transmitted orally. There is no doubt, at any rate, that in each of its hypostases, saying is superior to writing. The one-who-speaks requires a spiritual energy and a *continuity* of creative tension that may be lacking, and often is, in the one-who-writes.

"The one-who-speaks (leaving aside the vulgar, low specimen endowed or overendowed with that 'verve' through which the instinct of sociability manifests itself) imparts to *saying* his own inner lights, infusing and nurturing the painful flame of the ineffable with his own being. What one says is imbued with the sense of *what cannot be said*.

"Only when spoken can the word fulfill its profound *use* as a vehicle of revelation. Only speech can soar to the threshold beyond which alienation no longer holds sway. Writing is condemned to be a prisoner in the world of *having*. It is indeed fateful that we cannot *preserve* ourselves unless we accept *estrangement*: even our own selves are preserved only through self-estrangement. No doubt spoken language—insofar as it is a social act and presupposes, like any social act, a system of conventions—is not completely independent from the dialectics of estrangement. But there are moments—and it is to those, and only those, that I am now referring—when speech regains, as if by miracle, something of its original force of emanation, when it manages to recapture the *vocation* of sharing in the emanatory essence of the primordial Logos through which absolute being pronounced itself, revealed itself as Word. Any human language is impure, but the one-who-speaks places himself—in a virtual sense—much closer to the pure inaccessibility of being than the one-who-writes (no matter what he writes).

"Entrapped in the meshes of *having*, man managed to

intervene in the game of memory and forgetting by altering its natural balance. Writing appeared as a means of *conservation* (hence followed the entire vertiginous historical evolution, the geometrical progression of the ability to conserve, at all levels and in all fields, the diversification and refinement of individual or collective possessiveness). Initially conceived as a means of *lengthening memory*, writing brought about the tyranny of memory—but of an objectified, dehumanized memory that is drawn from the living rivers of forgetting and hardened into sign. Spoken words fly forth and are made to fly; written words remain and accumulate.

"The invention of writing marks the start of a process of corrupting human memory. In time, it is the sheet of paper covered with dead letters that must remember, must know, and must even think! Yes, as strange as it may seem, there are some who cannot even form thoughts without holding a pencil in hand before a blank sheet of paper. There are authors, slaves of the letter, who remain silent when asked what their books are about, remain mute and unruffled. After all, it suffices to read those books to discover what the books remember, what the books know, what the books think. In a way, one can say that *writing writes itself* while its author (a sort of sorcerer's apprentice) is simply a *medium* for conveying the boundless and unforeseeable complexity of its intentions.

"We can identify the seed of evil that writing offers such fertile soil"—Zacharias Lichter would say—"in memory itself. This happens even when memory has not yet alienated itself from the fluxes and refluxes of the primeval ocean of life-begetting forgetfulness. For memory is always animated by a secret will towards order and domination. It is endowed with the ability to fragment the whole and classify fragments according to their affinities, from contiguity to analogy and contrast. Thus, memory must be considered the *archetype of any power*. Here is not the place to talk about sacred powers or about the blessings of Remembering. But in social terms, it is not hard to see that a main characteristic of the development of humanity's political and economic organization was its effort to specialize and perfect (from the perspective of the *known*) all the processes and functions of memory. Writing and then printing were turning points on this road.

"All prejudice aside, how could one fail to see that the origins of writing are directly linked with the *imperatives of power*? The invention of writing—and this was in fact its primary aim—massively deepened the resources of oppression and exploitation. It facilitated or, better said, made possible the creation of large and stable empires and the tyrannical exercise of power in ever-larger social realms. Initially (and later in more hidden, subtler, and at the same time more efficient forms), writing was a *weapon* in the hands of power, a means of subjection and repression; a weapon and an instrument of torture of an invisible (and thus more savage, more monstrous) cruelty. From this perspective, writing meant a great victory for *having* and should be seen as a tragic event in the history of mankind, as the inauguration of an epoch in which human suffering (brought about by oppression) has recorded an unprecedented rise. If writing appears to us as a way of socializing memory—with the implications I have mentioned in passing—it is clear that *freedom*, on the social plane of course, can only be defined as an exit from history and as *forgetting*.

"One cannot say that people have ceased to forget. On the contrary, they forget more and more easily and lightheartedly, entrusting all they know, or imagine they know, to the sterile memory of the written word. Having lived for several millennia under the increasingly exclusive domination of the mechanisms of memory, constantly obsessed by an unnatural need for history and historicity, people seem to have forgotten even Forgetting itself. How many can still discern, behind the false axiology of dehumanized memory, the profound values of forgetting? How many can still *partake* of them?

"The one-who-speaks tends to reach, perhaps unawares, toward the sphere of these values. Indeed, when spoken language manages to rise above the practical, speech is *inspired* with being, shares in Being's eternal recurrence and loses itself in Being's eternal self-forgetting. The one-who-writes—and I have in mind here a *structure* that may be revealed even in those who are foreign to the various writing professions—also has access to forgetting: but to another kind of forgetting, which one indulges in as a 'reward,' in which one *settles down and sprawls* as in something *owned*, something soiled and debased by a sense of possession. The one-who-writes 'functionalizes' forgetting.

"Our world"—Zacharias Lichter went on—"can be compared to a huge book. We all wander willy-nilly through its pages, and our miserable beings are bloodied—to carry the metaphor further—by the endless brambles of the letters we are passing through. Even when we speak, it is as if we were reading aloud. On the other hand, it cannot be that what we say has not already been written. Everything has been written; everything has been turned into letter. We should not fool ourselves, but neither should we lose sight of our duty to try to rekindle, at all cost, the sacred flame of the primeval word. And when I say 'at all cost' I am thinking primarily of the painful cost of lying: a lying that (even when consubstantial with speaking) can only *hope* to find salvation in forgetting, in the all-begetting power of Forgetting. This forgetting—a fruit of perplexity—is our final purpose. In the spiritual order, stripped of the evils that accompanied its birth and multiplied in the course of its *evolution*, writing can only aspire, in the best of cases, to the accomplishment of various minor tasks. Spoken language may draw near to perplexity and—ideally—even partake in it. As far as I know, however, only the silence of Leopold Nacht *is in it*."

# ON THE MEANING OF LOVE

LEOPOLD Nacht had a younger sister, and through her he met an ugly and very modest young blond woman with whom he fell in love. His natural predisposition to silence was increased by the unknown and seemingly threatening new mood that was ravaging his being. Head drooping forward, chin hitting chest, with a fixed and empty gaze, Poldy would sit at a table—forgetting even his half-filled vodka glass—doing nothing for hours on end except grinding his teeth with a somber and dumbfounded air. He had not spoken a word in weeks—not even to Zacharias Lichter—and anyone who met him for the first time at this period would have been convinced they were dealing with an aphasiac.

The truth is that Leopold Nacht *did not need* to speak. Zacharias Lichter seemed to have become Leopold Nacht's spokesman. He would speak exclusively in his friend's name, devoting all his force of persuasion and resources of verbal incandescence to his service. Thus, in the end, he managed to dispel the blond girl's natural revulsion and fear of Nacht and convinced her that she was loved more than anyone ever had been loved or ever would be—loved more than anyone could dream. After a while the threesome—Nacht, Lichter, and the blond girl—were always seen together: the first, collapsed in his silent stupor; the girl, with a disoriented and sad air, silent herself; and between the two, the prophet, lips parched by the divine flame, eyes lit as if by an inner sun, speaking uninterruptedly and gesticulating wildly.

"Never was there a purer miracle of love"—Zacharias Lichter was saying. "For only the great Helpless One is granted the power of true love; and only the love of the great Barren One—which is constantly reborn yet ever the same— fulfills itself in pure fruition; and only the mouth of the great Silent One, from which even the memory of words has vanished, forms the Whole . . . We should prostrate ourselves at the feet of the divine Nacht and kiss the traces of his crooked and lame legs! Let us pray to the helpless, barren, silent Nacht! For he *is* the meaning of love."

# THE WANDERING JEW

PERIODICALLY, goaded by an irresistible impulse that could not be linked to any external cause, Zacharias Lichter would take off walking, holding himself erect and maintaining a mechanical rhythm of surprising steadiness, unable to stop for hours and sometimes even days on end. Thus he would suddenly depart, out of the blue, breaking off a conversation at some arbitrary point and leaving his interlocutor (if unaware of this trait) in a state akin to stupefaction. He would say goodbye with an uncomfortable smile, as if impelled by a force it would be useless to oppose, and stammer a hasty promise to continue the conversation "as soon as possible." And he would keep his promise, astonishing the uninformed interlocutor once again by picking up the thread of conversation, unflinchingly, without the slightest hesitation and with the most natural air in the world, exactly at the point where it had broken off.

The first thing he did upon falling prey to this "demon of perambulation" was to leave the city center. He was obscurely afraid and—as he would later confess—felt suddenly oppressed by a kind of curse. Moreover, he had the impression that he was awakening fright in others, that his suffocating anxiety might be contagious. He would thus retreat to less-populated areas on the outskirts of town, walking steadily, without looking right or left, yet with a sure sense of orientation, like a sleepwalker. (The comparison is quite apt since, when night fell, looking completely worn out, yet maintaining that monotonous rhythm that seemed to originate beyond time, his eyes would sometimes close and he would fall asleep, his face drawn tight by the terror of his oneiric visions.) There was something more curious, however: as he came to the end of some more or less labyrinthine road, his path would become circular and his silhouette could be seen circumambulating the same sordid urban area ten or even a hundred times, as if he could not extricate himself from that perimeter. In the end, the people in the neighborhood could not fail to note his haunting presence, which, after dark, seemed to exude an air of the occult and bizarre.

Absorbed in his own impenetrable world, Zacharias Lichter was of course totally unaware of all this. For him immediate reality had ceased to exist. When he returned to normal life, it was as if after a long trip: he displayed an absent, almost abstracted air, yet his gaze was limpid and intense, as if focused on vast spaces. When asked where he had been, Zacharias Lichter would answer as if in jest: "From time to time—out of sheer moral solidarity—I feel compelled to become again the Wandering Jew." And a faraway smile floated on his lips.

# THE METAPHYSICS OF
# LAUGHTER

As TIME went on—it was bound to happen—people started talking about Zacharias Lichter as a picturesque character, one of those "originals" whose deeds or unusual turns of phrase provoke amused interest or comic surprise, especially in that literary milieu where gossip at times acquires an intellectual tinge.

"Have you heard about Zacharias Lichter's latest folly? Let me tell you, it's incredible!" And amid bewildered exclamations and bursts of laughter, all sorts of strange stories and hilarious parables were told whose heroic protagonist—a hero seen as a combination of Diogenes, Nasreddin, and a Jewish prophet—was no other than Zacharias Lichter. For a long time he himself had no idea of the role his name and person was playing in the pseudo-folkloric anecdotes that animated the conversation, otherwise so banal and boring, of minor intellectual circles. He ended up, of course, learning about it but never gave any sign of being surprised or irritated, voicing deep satisfaction instead: "As I think more about it, it could not have happened otherwise. And on top of that, I recognize myself perfectly in this clown-like image. Didn't I start *to exist*, in a higher sense, when I realized my own condition as a clown? Haven't I tried to be a clown to the very end, unto madness? I would go so far as to say that the deeds and words that are attributed to me—be they funny, grotesque, or stupid—are in their essence truer than my own deeds and words . . . And of course they do not realize, narrow-minded as they are, that by laughing at me they come close—too dangerously so for their own stupidity—to the profound core of my thinking. They don't realize that, objectively, their laughter gains a metaphysical dimension: so that a keen mind, even starting from as low a level as the manner and nuances of their laughter, could reconstruct the paradoxical edifice of my philosophy, illuminated by the great lightning bolt of Revelation.

"A prophet can frighten, can set off an earthquake in hearts; but he is never closer to achieving his mission than when he becomes the object of ridicule. For in the laughter he arouses (irrespective of his motives, which could be real or false), the world whose decline he prophesied *effectively collapses* . . . Laughter purifies like a sacred flame. But only the madmen, the prophets and the saints *know* that—and that is why they make efforts to make the entire universe roar with laughter, until the stars tremble. My only regret is that until now I could make so few people laugh at me; and that, when I laugh *at myself*, my laughter is louder than everyone else's. Could this be the sign of my failure?"

And, before any of those to whom he was speaking could start to laugh, Zacharias Lichter burst out, with suddenly congested face and bloodshot eyes, in long, strange, and frightening peals of laughter.

# LEGENDS

As mentioned in the previous fragment, all sorts of legends grew up around Zacharias Lichter. The laughter they provoked in certain circles was hearty and even greedy for more, a laughter in which—as the derided prophet himself suggested—a finely tuned ear could have discerned echoes of emptiness, the first signs of a world trembling on the brink of apocalyptic collapse; but also the first signs of an apotheosis.

One cycle of legends concerned Lichter's sexual behavior.

A self-styled former college friend, it seems, was the source of certain tales about Lichter's supposedly hyperbolic sexuality, which unfolded exclusively on a cosmic plane. Lichter thought of himself, according to this fanciful testimony, as an embodiment of absolute virility and was said to be obsessed by the feminine principle found everywhere in nature. He thus yearned to copulate with all primordial elements, with the oceans and with the earth, with the starry firmament and with fire. At the sight of any of these he was seized with irresistible centauresque urges.

Along this same line, an older episode from one of his trips to the seaside was reported by the so-called former college friend as follows: Zacharias Lichter sat for an entire day on the beach with the sun beating down on his head, seemingly dazed. By chance, but perhaps not entirely so, he was situated near a rocky outcrop where nudist women sought what shelter they could while sunbathing. Towards evening a few of them were still there, going to and from the sea with languid movements, their breasts and hips swaying, water glittering like silver on their tanned skin. Lichter was not watching them, however; with piercing eyes, he was peering out into the distance, scanning the monotonous ripples of the sea emanating from the curved horizon. From time to time, as if possessed, he would start to run, heavily and off-balance, yet seemingly driven by a force and energy about to be unleashed at any moment—toward the metallic highlights playing on the waves as the sun descended. He would throw himself brusquely into the sea, emitting strange cries of pleasure, swirling and thrashing about in the throes of a mixture of lust and ferocity, totally oblivious to what was going on around him. When he emerged again, water streaming down his broad, hairy chest, eyes shining feverishly, his whole being seemed charged with raw, unrestrained vigor. On his final return, he emerged from the sea shouting and began to roll in the sand while still dripping wet, tossing about spasmodically for a time like some amphibious monster in the throes of a sexual act. All this beneath the frightened stares of those still remaining on the beach in the cooling twilight. Even the few nudists, covering their nakedness with their arms, looked on in fascination as the incredible scene unfolded. Everything lasted barely a few minutes. Then, totally spent and emptied of all energy, Lichter lay for some time seemingly unconscious, his inert body covered with coarse patches of sand. Much later, as if released by a spring, he jumped up, grabbed his clothes with an automatic gesture, and bolted away like some frightened object of prey, as ridiculous as it seemed in the tranquility reigning that evening on the beach, broken only by the calm flight of seagulls and the swirl of rippling waves. Lichter—his former classmate explained, not without a certain wicked aesthetic delight—feared the intensity of the erotic impulses generated in him by the grandiose spectacle of nature, which is why he so seldom left town. Given his cosmic sexuality, urban life was a form of abstinence and asceticism.

There were others who lowered the level of the gossip still further. They ignored the legends regarding Lichter's cosmic sexuality—legends in which, by the way, one can easily discern a form of mockery through exaggeration—and spread rumors that behind his mask of theoretical disinterest in the erotic, Lichter engaged in strange clandestine activities in that very area. Lacking any true vocation for asceticism, he took great pains to hide his passionate interest in women, regardless of their social status. They cited adventures with a gypsy beggar, with an old crone who cleaned street urinals, and with a snobbish intellectual who practiced theosophy. All these tales repeatedly emphasized—in a depressingly vulgar way—the contrast between Lichter's professed ideals and his actual practice. Thus he was reportedly seen on a park bench with a young street-sweeper on his lap, initiating her into the principles of Ecstatics or existential Dilemmatics (disciplines he had *in fact* founded), while pausing from time to time to cover her face with wild, passionate kisses.

According to others—whether he had stated it openly or not—Lichter had discovered a mystical value in eroticism, a portal to Perplexity. Thus he not only refused to oppose his basic instincts but stimulated them in every possible area, including the culinary: believing that garlic possessed aphrodisiac qualities, Lichter consumed great quantities of it, as a result of which—here they were obviously striving for

a crude comic effect—women found him repulsive and refused to come near him. This plunged Lichter into states of
extreme frustration, leading to murky prophesies and bursts
of metaphysical hysteria.

Another cycle of legends arose around Zacharias Lichter's
inexplicable "flights," in which he would run about aimlessly.
It was said, for example, that before such a flight, he would
go through a preliminary stage characterized by a sort of
"aura," a quite lengthy period that sometimes lasted up to a
week or more. To designate this period, the bizarre (and no
doubt ungainly) term of *folfa* was attributed to Lichter.* At
such times, he would fall into a sort of prostration, interrupted now and then by bursts of verbal delirium, the inco-
herence of which made those around him feel as if they were
participating in some sort of weird rite. It was said that
during *folfa* Lichter proved exceptionally receptive to intel-

---

*A philologist offered an elegant explanation of this term, unrecorded in dic-
tionaries. According to his hypothesis, *folfa* describes a concealed agitation, a
flood of anxiety, the onset of a state of possession. It points, on the one hand,
toward a strong inner sensation of "fluttering" (the constellation *flt* presenting
a striking parallel to the term under discussion), a strange sense of sluggish
flight through thick ooze. On the other hand, *folfa* is associated with increased
difficulty of self-expression, with words stammered out in a "snuffling" language (here again, the phonetic similarities with *folfa* were obvious). Enlarging
upon these preliminary remarks, the philologist developed—to the amusement of the gathering—a sort of an ironic ontology of *folfa*. He discovered in it
one of the fundamental hypostases of *being* in confrontation with *nonbeing*. A
philosopher contradicted the philologist however, maintaining that *folfa*
might merely be a state of existential stupor. There were others who claimed
that Lichter staged his "folfas," thus repudiating his status as a Judaic prophet
and revealing his hidden connections with various Eastern religions. Several
anecdotes were told along these lines, among which was the following: In response to a question on the nature of God, Lichter asked his interlocutor to
spit on him—and when the latter refused to do so, implored him again, nearly
in tears. Following this, the prophet fell into a state of *folfa*. The man understood and left the room, overcome by humility…

lectual matters. Although he responded only with grunts and snorts and made not the slightest gesture, while his face retained the blank stare of a cretin, he remembered all that was said to him with great accuracy, so that when his "flight" was over, he could weave into subsequent discussions, ardently and with his usual acuity, everything he had left unanswered during those perplexed days of *folfa*. It was also reported that his students, realizing this—and aware of Lichter's notorious tendency towards endless monologues—took advantage of his *folfas* to broach their own ideas, formulate their questions, clear up confusions, and even raise objections.

All these accounts—peppered to various extents with racy details according to the talent of the teller—provoked enormous roars of laughter. But this very laughter—as we have seen—carried for Lichter a purifying value. In time, and without substantively modifying his initial reaction, he began to speak of a *Calvary of the Grotesque and the Picturesque*.

"Ridicule"—Zacharias Lichter would say—"of whatever kind, should be *assumed*; just as sin, lies, suffering, life, or death may be assumed—no matter their nature. Purity assumes filth and vulgarity. Chastity assumes the raptures of desire, for they are part and parcel of chastity, just as filth is of purity, stupidity of wisdom, stammering of elocution. So ridicule too is part and parcel of the serious.

"Without being anywhere, God may flare up in anything, at any place. His flame unifies the laughter and tears of mankind. It delivers us from the narrow game of meaning. Thus we must be willing to signify all things: to pass, with equal goodwill, for angels or monsters, for saints or laughingstocks, for ourselves or others. For all things draw us toward God more rapidly, more clearly, more beautifully, even those we find difficult to accept…

"On the way towards God, we have to climb several mountains in turn, and among them is the burning mountain of Laughter. The test of fire: the test of laughter.

"This is my prayer: Make them, O God, laugh at me; may they grant me the charity of their laughter. Give me, O God, the strength to *be* the same one who *appears* in their laughter. And let their fiery clamor wash me clean. Let not my legs tremble on that climb, sharp as flint, through the scorching heat of my ugliness. And let not my mind falter. Let not my love waver ... "

As he was saying this, Zacharias Lichter's eyes glistened as if brightened by tears.

# ON RETICENCE

G. HAD A thin yet harsh voice, with plaintive drawn-out tones like sobbing prayers. From his mouth, filled with broken and darkened teeth barely held in place by the rotting gums, words emerged with difficulty, as if drawn forth from some obscure ancient despondency—even with regard to the most everyday things and circumstances.

He also had a singular way of remaining silent—an attentive silence, filled with tense expectation. A silence that drew in and absorbed all that others said, robbing them of their verbal resources, placing them in a surprising and baffling predicament, pierced by a gaze that flickered with a strange mixture of coldness, bemusement, and intense dreaminess.

In the noisy hell of taverns, where he spent much of his time (though he was no alcoholic), G. kept so quiet and at the same time so near the threshold of speech that words seemed ready to burst forth at any moment, storming all barriers. Yet that did not happen. He would only start talking much later, after downing a good number of glasses, dolefully lengthening each syllable, his small hands with uncut nails making slow, distinctive gestures that always seemed to be weighing invisible objects. Anyone who followed the intermittent thread of his phrases closely would develop in time a clear sense that each uttered word, like his gestures, was weighing, with trepidation and great care, its own meaning: the weight of that meaning.

With his thirty-some years, G. presented the figure of a wise man, an intransigent moralist who harbored no illusions about human nature. He liked to think of himself, without excessive vanity and even with certain dignified modesty, as a man who had the right to judge others, as an administrator of justice—exclusively in the theoretical realm, it seems.

It is in this capacity that he was consulted (perhaps at first with a certain irony, which nonetheless slowly but surely faded away) on various moral questions, to which he generally offered the sternest of solutions. Curiously, although he resorted to a rather obvious rhetoric (rhetoric, as we know, being the child of moralism), his unwieldy, quivering replies—uttered in a voice that rose to an unbelievably high register, only to immediately break and expire in a sort of a wheeze, then begin its ascension anew, again and again, followed by the same sudden break and fall, like some mechanical form of weeping—had the effect of deepening the spiritual atmosphere his long previous silence had imposed. Imperceptibly, those at the table, struck dumb, would find themselves in a zone of such severity and paralyzing rigor that the slightest smile would have seemed unpardonably rude.

G.'s encounter with Zacharias Lichter (through the agency of Leopold Nacht) constituted a turning point in the former's life.

From time to time, late in the evening, G. would evoke this decisive moment:

"Zacharias Lichter devastated me by ferreting out a sense of metaphysical shame . . . *the shame of existing.* A crushing, stifling, maddening shame. In his proximity I felt ashamed, for instance, that I was ever thirsty or even hungry. We were in some dive once and I wanted something to eat; I asked him what he would like, but he didn't order anything... It's always unpleasant to eat in front of someone else, but I will never forget how thoroughly abject I felt at that moment, how deeply I loathed my own hunger and the food my body craved, an aversion that increased when I found I could not satisfy my hunger. On the contrary, it grew ever greater, turned ravenous, intoxicating, maddening... And all this while listening to Zacharias Lichter's abstract discourse on the devouring Flame...

"In his presence I felt ashamed of anything that might bring me pleasure. His world seemed to have exiled even the most innocent of joys (a sweeping landscape, the scent of a flower, a butterfly's flickering flight). And not only that: the same shame gripped me with regard to all my sorrows, my pains, my dilemmas, which now seemed grotesquely trivial, worthy only of scorn. Existence was emptied of all charm, of all beauty, no matter how slight; being was reduced to its frightening nakedness. Only one thing retained any meaning: suffering. Not of the moral sort (always prey to self-indulgence) but suffering which penetrates the flesh like a tongue of flame: physical pain, illness..."

After a while G. began to avoid Zacharias Lichter. At the same time, he abandoned his former intransigence (his entire "righteousness complex" had dissipated) and now practiced a sort of constantly compassionate humility. "God"—he used to say—"dwells not only in sorrow and heartbreak but also in the smallest luminous aspects of existence. It is there that we should seek him, in the joy we find in the trembling of grass or in the flight of birds. Existence itself should fill us with deep gratitude, in whatever form it manifests itself.

When we grow ashamed of our innocent joys, desires, nostalgia, and even suffering, our souls run the risk of becoming seriously ill, and we should take preventive measures. No matter how much we may believe that on those occasions we draw closer to God, in reality we are as far as possible from the breath of His goodness."

Without altering his mode of existence, G. had changed. His silences, as long as ever, had lost their secret power to baffle, suggesting instead an endless patience. His words, still drawling and plaintive, no longer imposed an atmosphere of severity and rigor: instead they emanated an aura of kind and generous emotion. On nights feebly illuminated by dirty bulbs, amid the noise and dense smoke of the taverns he frequented, G. radiated a spirit of reconciliation and even meekness. His states of inebriation were luminous and calm: angels and butterflies drifted by. Butterflies in particular obsessed him at such times—everything centered on them, to the exclusion of all other winged species...

Zacharias Lichter spoke of him with a certain affection, although he had noticed that G. was avoiding him.

"His discovery—to which I may have contributed myself, unwittingly, as is often the case—is that one can also find one's path to *being* through *reticence*. His condition perfectly illustrates what one might call the dialectics of *suavizare*, an intermediary form between circus and madness. Circus is subject, from that perspective, to a *suave* contemplation that both smooths and soothes: the most awkward and grotesque movements of the clowns, when slowed down, assume the nature of ineffably pure drifting flight; accelerated, they begin to resemble those fluttering butterflies G. sometimes seems to see everywhere. The dialectics of *suavizare* is not based on affirmation and negation, nor does it enter the sterile circuit of identity and opposition, its terms are beyond language, *in the vision*, the slowing down and the acceleration: everything becomes slower and at the same time faster. Everything floats and flies, emptied of all immanence... And then, we begin to love everything, comprehend everything, become reticent before everything; and the place we are within the circus becomes *the center of the world's reticence.* Reticence cannot be learned, of course; it is a secret road, a vocation, just as all vocations are secret roads. It is no less true, however, that reticence will finally prove to be a weakness, because its path does not end in madness but merely in beautiful games of deception."

Whenever he caught sight of Zacharias Lichter or heard his name mentioned, G. would drill his incredibly shrill voice into someone's ear, breaking off as usual with a screech on the final syllables: "Poor fellow! I pity him to no end."

# AGAIN ON "ANALYSIS"

IN HIS relations with Zacharias Lichter—limited relations, in point of fact, because the prophet did all in his power to avoid him—Doctor S. experimented, with a perfidious discretion, a kind of "maieutics of the known." In a casual and relaxed manner, he would drop phrases here and there whose secret sense he alone knew, in an attempt to make Zacharias define himself, as it were, of his own accord.

For anyone other than S., it would have been difficult if not impossible to apply this procedure, since Lichter put so much passion into any conversation that it soon turned into a monologue, as forceful as a cascade. His interlocutor then had the sensation (purely intellectual, of course) that he could not *hear* his own words and, given the abstract roar produced by the waterfall of the prophet's speech, silence imposed itself as the only natural attitude. But Doctor S. struck such terror in Zacharias Lichter that he spontaneously adopted a defensive stance, taking refuge in the horizonless space of simple replies. Thus, without asserting his power through dynamic gestures and encountering no resistance, Doctor S. would gain mastery over the situation, while Lichter, in a state of increasing confusion, would be transformed into a simple subject of psychological investigation, while remaining painfully aware of what was happening to him.

"*Domnule* Lichter"—Doctor S. addressed him when they

once chanced to meet on the street—"I must confess or, rather, repeat an older confession which, alas, has remained without consequence: it would give me great pleasure to talk with you at greater length, to get to know you better. But I have the impression that you're avoiding me. You seem to harbor a certain reserve toward me, as if something about me or my conduct displeases you, though I'm not exactly sure what..."

"My reserve"—Lichter answered, drawing back quickly— "if indeed it exists at all, has another source: we are, in fact, fundamentally dissimilar, and I feel it would be impossible for us to communicate in any other way other than the conventional..."

"But this is exactly what attracts me to you! And besides, let me put my cards on the table: in my profession I have met any number of religious maniacs, prophets, paranoid reformers, and schizophrenics who have fallen into mystical contemplation—a multitude of varied cases, but all, in the final analysis, depressingly banal. It's perfectly normal that I want to know a true mystic at last, and a profound thinker as well, which you are said to be..." And a benevolent smile fluttered on the psychiatrist's thin lips.

"Are the cases you mention as banal as all that? It seems to me, on the contrary, that madness is the very opposite of banality. No, even more, that when facing the enigmatic reality of madness, the notion of banality empties itself of meaning..."

"Well, after all," Doctor S. replied, "any science is, in a sense, a search for the banal. What enters its radar are phenomena of repetition, recurrent series, the 'ordinary,' if you like..."

"But, Doctor"—Lichter interrupted him, stammering

humbly—"madness . . . is something else altogether. One must grasp it, not explain it. It is not we who are called to explain it but, rather, it is madness that explains us—and not in the usual sense of the word but in the etymological one. Even unknowingly, we are all simply *unfoldings* of madness . . ."

As he would later report, Lichter felt at that moment an obscure yet powerful urge to rehabilitate madness in the eyes of that dry psychiatrist, who had seemingly ceased being a person and turned into a *symbol* (of cold sterility, of methodic cruelty, of sadistic lucidity which, in order to analyze, destroys what is unique and breaks it down into its component parts, consigning the fragments torn from the living whole to the mortuary caskets of the known). If he could, he would have sacrificed himself to ennoble the idea of madness, to enfold it, if only for a moment, in the mystery whose carrier he was. A desire gripped him to go mad himself in what would seem the most banal sense. In this way, and only this way, he believed, he could break through the rigid crust of banality in Doctor S.'s eyes. He would bring the doctor face to face—perhaps in awe and terror—with the sacred and paradoxical essence of madness. But at the same time Lichter knew that he was prey to a *temptation*, that his sacrifice would simply be a self-deception, and Doctor S., far from having a revelation, would be *confirmed* and strengthened in his convictions. In spite of this, the temptation was growing stronger.

"And what if I myself"—he said, with a haggard air—"if I were . . . or actually am, truly mad? As a matter of fact, *I am mad*, mad beyond doubt—and I am amazed that you did not notice it from the start. I am the Messiah—the Savior of all madmen past and future, their embodied hope, their revealed mystery. Look me straight in the eye, Doctor, and stop pretending: you *know* everything."

Eyes sparkling with icy curiosity, Doctor S. had carefully watched Lichter, who seemed to have slipped into a state of euphoria; yet at the same time, Lichter was overcome by the strange (and unsettling) feeling that rather than vexing the psychiatrist, he had merely been fulfilling indirectly, even systematically, *all his expectations*. It was as if these expectations, though not explicitly, had the secret power to induce in him gestures, attitudes and thought processes increasingly incompatible with his deepest nature. And Lichter felt that everything was being taken from him, that the doctor's analytical expectations were dissecting, one by one, all his thoughts, all his gestures, appropriating them and leaving him empty.

"That is not possible"—Doctor S. smiled amiably— "although, after all . . . Obviously, anything is possible. If so, you would be a madman aware of his own madness, something not infrequent in superior individuals. Well then—since we are already playing the game—let's take advantage of your lucidity: how does it manifest itself, in more precise terms, this madness you maintain you suffer from?"

"I hear God's flame, I see it, I feel it burning. From its midst a voice sometimes speaks to me: 'You are a whirligig'—it cries, and I start spinning and whistling until I fall down in a daze; 'You are a horse'—and I begin tramping and neighing; 'You are a stone'—and I freeze where I am . . . My madness can assume all the forms of existing madness: that is why I proclaim myself the Messiah of madmen . . ."

Doctor S. was listening to Lichter with sustained attention, piercing him with his gaze. He was not incognizant of the fact that Lichter was saying, at random, whatever passed through his mind, that *for the time being* he was pretending—that did not surprise him at all; for there are lunatics who try—and Zacharias Lichter knew this himself—to hide their madness, often with naive cunning. They become actors of a sort, playing the role of other madmen or even of normal people. But even from this game, from the type of mental associations on which it relies, from details of its particulars, a fine diagnostician can deduce to which category the madman in fact belongs.

"Interesting"—Doctor S. muttered—"extremely interesting…"

Lichter had an immediate sense of acute danger. Whatever he did, whatever he said (whether he was sincere or played some arbitrary character invented ad hoc), he became a sign within a system of signs whose code belonged only to the doctor; and this irreversible codification of his sentient being so alienated him from himself that all he was mimicking ended up appearing to him more real than it actually was.

Without saying goodbye, face darkened and gaze misty, Zacharias Lichter bolted into a disorderly run. Still, not even that was apt to surprise the doctor, who continued on his way, engrossed in thought. This flight—Lichter later realized—was for the psychiatrist yet one more sign. Lichter could not conjecture its meaning but felt, somehow, impoverished, left with a curious sense of *lack*, an inner void.

# THE SIGNIFICANCE OF
# THE MASK

"In the crucial moments of our rapport with others we should be wearing masks," Zacharias Lichter was telling his friends, "for only the mask can express the true dialectics of the spirit with all its inner tensions. Physiognomy has significance only on the psychological plane; the mask places its wearer, unaware as he may be, within the ontological sphere.

"The mask's paradox comes from the fact that it *shows*, it *indicates*, but at the same time it *conceals*. At times it indicates the very thing it conceals, revealing its essence, incorporated however, in one or another of its grotesque archetypes. At other times, this rapport can be inverted: the essence is hidden, ushered into the 'category of the secret.' In both cases, however, the mask—by negating the pseudocomplexity of the psychological—constitutes the first means of voluntarily accessing the spiritual. By what the mask shows or hides, the wearer defends himself, with the aid of the enigmatic, against the danger of *alienation*. He offers himself to endless deciphering, mocking at the same time all such attempts . . .

"Society, whose cohesion is based on the very *alienation* of the individuals who constitute it, has in time instituted false values in whose name not only the mask but the very idea of the mask has been depreciated and minimized to such an extent that the mask, with rare exceptions, is exiled even from the theater. Yet the spirit manages to create, by the most unlikely means, the masks it needs to defend itself. Thus some great poets have turned words themselves into masks.

"As for me,"—Zacharias Lichter explained—"I have managed to turn my own face into a mask. Undoubtedly I was helped by what everyone considers my loathsome, monstrous ugliness. Because—have you noticed?—in the first place, a mask needs to be *ugly*—or so social conventions teach us . . . But what is ugliness? The pain that we fear is ugly; the laughter we fear is ugly, the truth we fear is ugly. Well, *I* am all these. And that is why my face is not simply a mask, but the *mask of masks*."

# ON HASTE

HASTE seems to Zacharias Lichter among the most pernicious modalities of sin: he who hurries intellectualizes the world, dries up all that is living, and ushers in devastation and death.

Put most simply, haste is the desire to reach a goal more quickly. It is, in other words, a paroxystic form of the consciousness of time but also a revolt against time: since it is in theory *infinite*, it tends to abolish time. It is under these conditions that the dialogue between the man in a hurry and his goal occurs. Due to the effect of *preventive resentment*,* the goal appears to the man in a hurry as small and negligible; on the other hand, through his haste, he invests it with singular importance, thus deluding himself twice. This situation engenders a *dialectics of falsification*. In the name of a goal located somewhere in the abstract future, the man

---

*Zacharias Lichter distinguishes between *resentment per se* (which appears when a desire is condemned to remain unfulfilled, excellently illustrated in the classic fable of the fox and the grapes) and *preventive resentment*, which manifests itself when the fulfillment of a desire is possible but not certain. On the path desire takes towards satisfaction (assuming that the latter is neither simple nor immediate), in case of actual failure preventive resentment, which is a form of caution, opens the way for resentment per se. When the goal is difficult to attain, preventive resentment may become strong enough to turn into resentment per se long before failure becomes certain. All those who habitually fail suffer from a hypertrophy of preventive resentment, an attribute, in most cases, of more cerebral natures.

in a hurry suspends the present, the real, and the concrete, leaving them prey to the permeable force of an empty past that ultimately is nothing but the inversion, equally abstract, of the future.

In its essence, haste *is a game* (in the mathematical sense) of abstractions; an algebra of the unreal superimposed upon the extant; a summing up of the world in purely temporal equations...

On a human plane, haste reverses the natural relation between path and goal. It is by now a commonplace to say that the path towards a goal is more precious than the goal itself, the latter appearing, in the end, merely as an occasion for structuring this experience in subsequent representations. An attained goal—no matter of what kind—has no other value than the one presented by the path taken towards it; in this sense, the man in a hurry never attains his goals because he neglects the very paths that lead to them. The man in haste wanders through an endless desert for all eternity. Under his gaze everything turns to sand: thus, in his mad haste, lacking any landmarks, he actually runs in place.

To be in a hurry—Zacharias Lichter maintains—means either to hate the world or fail to love it—which comes to the same thing.

He who hurries hastens to die.

He who dies brings death to the world.

That is why haste is such a great sin...

# FROM THE POEMS OF ZACHARIAS LICHTER

In time, we die.
We hasten to die.
In night, we darken.
And we darken the world.
Thirst is the only light.
*There* nothing is spoken.
The word is sipped in silence.
In rain.
In God.

# ON ILLNESS

IN SPITE of his robust constitution, Zacharias Lichter is sometimes taken ill. Harsh winters in particular, with bouts of bitter, extreme cold, test his health severely, no matter how hardened he has become by his life as a beggar (stuffing old newspapers under his shirt proved futile). Trembling with fever, eyes burning, barely able to drag his feet along, exhausted by the throbbing, painful burden of his own body, Lichter bore his illness with him as he wandered the freezing streets, whipped by cutting winds. "Home" would have been an even more dangerous place to be. He might have frozen stiff in his run-down, unheated garage, where snow whirled almost as strongly inside as out during blizzards. Besides, walking warmed him, and in the end that painful, almost inhuman effort, extended for one more moment and then another, assured him that he had not yet reached the limits of his endurance. And thus, without changing his regular habits, the prophet recovered miraculously, his erstwhile wavering steps regained their strength, and his bent figure emanated once more an air of strange energy, abstract yet responsive.

On no account would he see a doctor, for he regarded illness as perfectly natural, and thus never complained about it. If he mentioned in passing that he was ill, he did so solely to warn those with whom he came in contact that he might be contagious. The terror Doctor S. awoke in him seemed to extend (albeit in a much attenuated form) to all representatives of the medical profession, regardless of their field. "From a certain age on," he used to say, taking up again an earlier observation, "we each become our own best doctor, in the most *practical* sense: we know what agrees with our body and what doesn't, what helps us recover and what only aggravates the illness." On the other hand, Lichter considered *fear of illness* much more damaging than illness itself. He believed that modern society suffers from a true psychosis of prophylaxis: starting from a number of erroneous presuppositions, society inevitably arrived at even more erroneous conclusions that were nearly dizzying to those who approached them with clear reasoning or even simple "common sense."

"Cleanliness has thus lost any ritualistic meaning," Zacharias Lichter would point out, "rather than a participation in the essence of purity, as it once was, it has been transformed into a mere precautionary hygienic measure. Now there is even a tendency to 'explain' (in the grossly distorting vision of the history of religions) the various cultic obligations, interdictions, and recommendations as sanitary measures dressed in religious garb in order to gain greater authority in backward societies dominated by a superstitious-magical mentality. Thus, for instance"—Lichter could multiply the examples at will—"the various food exclusions, and fasting itself, are today interpreted as empirical prescriptions, belonging to the prehistory of modern nutrition regimens. And it is forgotten that, after all, not what was forbidden or prescribed was of importance (in that regard, no matter how we look at things, we find ourselves in the realm of the completely arbitrary). What counted was the *existence* of a rigorous system of interdictions and sanctions with a purely ritualistic value. Their observance *made possible* (only possible, never certain, because in this domain the mechanical relations established by scientific intellect have no place) an ineffable intimacy with the sacred.

"In the Realm of Stupidity"—Zacharias Lichter was saying—"an entire intellectual category distinguishes itself by what could be called *inventiveness in the sphere of illness*, and this inventiveness is often of an extraordinary acuity. Here we have, undoubtedly, a consequence of the mistaken conception (in this case mistaken and guilty are one and the same) regarding the normal state, the essence of normality. In the Realm of Stupidity, a *normal* condition and access to it imply sacrificing individuality (*abnormal*, by definition). Health has become a norm, an ideal even, and illness has totally lost its paradoxical value, its capacity to express *the natural and the lack of meaning of the natural*.

"A real chasm has opened between health and illness. The opposition between the spiritual and the nonspiritual has also been replaced by, among other specious oppositions, that of health vs. illness, which accords so well with the requirements devised by the practical spirit. Imperceptibly—and not surprisingly—a kind of a debased religion of health, of 'normality,' has been created, obsessed with the problem of illness. Thus, besides those known for ages, thousands and tens of thousands of illnesses, one more complicated than the other, have been *invented* and along with them, equally complicated means of combatting them. And this merely in the name of health and the repugnantly abstract idolatry of health as a goal in itself. The vast, precious experience of illness and suffering which, in its own way, every religion of the world sought to keep and pass on, is dissipated and lost without trace. (Think again of Job, of his chaste body covered with boils and pus, of the innumerable excruciating torments that have shaped Job's ever-questioning wisdom.)

"Open sores, festering boils, a racing pulse, the eyes rolled back, their light turned inward, the shaking, the desperate cries of the ill, pain or the absence of pain, delirium or clear-mindedness are today nothing more than *symptoms*, more or less manifest, more or less 'characteristic.' The codification of all these symptoms, their systematization into an over-confident *semiology* (doubled by an etiology and a therapeutics that are equally variable, equally hypothetical, in spite of all the practical results) have contributed to the transformation of medicine into a 'science' that measures its progress through statistics recording efficiency. Lowering the coefficient of mortality, extending the average life span—these are the great prides of modern science, to which may soon be added genetic control, eugenics, euthanasia and even—why not?—the artificial replication of human life. Everything, of course, in the name of Man, based on the irrefutable arguments of *scientific morality*.

"How can we fail to see that medicine, along with the other more or less related branches of biological science, is nothing but a serious malady? That, together with the life sciences as a whole, medicine does nothing but dissect life, reduce it to its components, decompose it, and while recomposing it, estrange it from its mysterious and holy sources, falsifying and further degrading it? That we are facing an extremely dangerous attempt to de-spiritualize life? That we are witnessing an attempt to replace life with mere simulacra?

"In fact"—Zacharias Lichter went on—"in the Realm of Stupidity, what medicine proposes is not to *understand* suffering and illness as phenomena of real life, and not even to *alleviate* them: the goals of the medicine are 'reproductive' (one seeks to reproduce the physical and psychical state anterior to illness by doing one's best to eradicate all its traces and consequences, even the consciousness of having been ill) and quantitative-statistical. That we could *learn* something from illness that does not accord with the known, that by contemplating life threatened by death we could extract a lesson, a sense of sanctity, an ineffable mystery, nothing is more alien to these goals than the present profession of medicine. They have forgotten, alas, that the true healer must love the one who suffers, must love his unique illness, must study his disease until he experiences it himself, until he *partakes* in the weakness, the fear, the agony and wisdom of the sick, even in their approaching death. They have forgotten, alas, that the true healer must not convince the one who is sick of the efficacies of his remedies and advice, but convince the sufferer to return his love: by sharing his strength, his confidence, his well-being and naiveté, and even his death, which is still far off and will perhaps be gentler and more serene. One other important thing the true healer must do: prevent the one who suffers from forgetting…

"If we leave aside its grand ambitions and the great perils born of them, medicine remains a trade that can be practiced with greater or lesser professional integrity; a trade that aims to *restore* the patient, to *reinstate* him to his exact condition prior to the illness, or to a condition as close as possible to it. Medical practice, seen as a social effort (the purpose of which, in the final analysis, is to restore the patient's productive capacity), participates in the game of economic values and, as such, receives its remuneration. Thus it clearly falls into the realm of *having*. Yet healing can be only an act of love, a manifestation of being, even if it utilizes one or another of the means supplied by medicine. The goal of healing is altogether different: the healer does not dispel illness but takes it unto himself; recovery does not appear as the result of science but—as in fact it has always been—as a miracle."

Several times, when Leopold Nacht had fallen gravely ill, Lichter himself watched over him, caring for him with utter dedication, never leaving his bedside. Moreover, he did for his friend what he would never have done for himself: he called a doctor and scrupulously followed his prescriptions.

# ON MIRRORS

Zacharias Lichter's handful of initiates were concerned about the turn his friendship with Leopold Nacht was taking. Indeed, for some time now, Lichter could no longer talk without bringing up Nacht, commenting on his silences or gestures, with no apparent reference to their meaning, or rather lack of meaning. Thus once, when Nacht was drunk—nothing is more predictable in such circumstances—he broke out in a meaningless rage. Groaning and gnashing his teeth, he threw his glass, still half-filled with vodka, at the greasy mirror of the tavern, slanted just above the table at which he sat with Zacharias Lichter. The mirror did not break, but the drinking glass shattered, attracting the attention—in spite of the general hubbub—of a few clients at neighboring tables. Turning his rage upon himself, Nacht suddenly grabbed a knife—one of those dull knives found in common taverns, with a gray, soiled blade—and quickly thrust it, with almost incredible force, through his left hand, which was lying palm-up upon the table; the blow was so strong that the blade penetrated to the wood.

Profoundly shaken, Zacharias Lichter later explained: "In attempting to break the mirror, Nacht was trying—desperately—to institute paradisiac knowledge. He wished to break all the mirrors of the world by means of which we are condemned to *guess* our faces. He wanted to destroy illusion and proclaim the triumph of *seeing*: face to face. But he did not succeed. Are we to remain in reflection's bondage then— how long? how long? And who will free us from the world of mirrors? Nacht's failure must have seemed absolute. That is why he felt the need to punish himself, to thrust the knife through the hand that failed. I will never forget, when he pulled out the knife, how blood spread like a red lily in his palm. I could not help but kiss Nacht's bloody hand. Even now I can taste his blood in my mouth; it tastes of metal, of earth, and of resurrection."

That evening Poldy got so drunk that Lichter had to carry him on his back to the nearest park. He laid him down on a bench, covered him with his own jacket, and watched over him till dawn . . .

# INNOCENCE AND GUILT

ON ONE occasion, Zacharias Lichter disappeared and did not return for several weeks. The absence was too long to be attributed to one of his enigmatic "flights." On his return, his acquaintances were baffled to hear that he had been detained by the police on a charge of theft—a charge against which, although innocent, he had not protested. They only released him when, by sheer chance, they caught the real thief. Even then Lichter said nothing, not did he complain of the brutal treatment he had been subjected to, like any ordinary criminal, during detention.

"What was I to do?" Zacharias Lichter explained. "It's extremely disagreeable to be unjustly accused, but it's much more *unpleasant*—and the term seems to me too weak—to have to proclaim one's innocence. For truly there is something odious and profoundly indecent in every attempt to deny guilt. Had I been sentenced to ten years in prison for a crime I'd never dreamt of, I still would have not demeaned myself to prove my innocence. Even if I'd been threatened with being burnt at the stake for an idea I did not share—an idea that seemed to me false, fallacious, or repellent—I would have preferred to be a martyr in its name than make an effort to disavow it.

"Claiming one's innocence (no matter how justified) is ultimately demeaning because it always seems dictated by a cowardly acceptance of the accuser's criteria. In such a case, innocence is no longer the absence of guilt but fuses with mere lack of sufficient evidence of guilt. Innocence is degraded to the point of being reduced to an *alibi* (imagine a *saint*, a victim of the inquisitor's error or animus, being forced to resort to alibis! It is absurd! He will accept any accusation, even of having made a pact with the devil, because *the essence of any accusation is that it is always justified*). Actually, nothing is clearer: purity cannot, should not be proved. Attempting to do so negates purity, irreversibly soils it. No matter what crime you stand accused of, defending yourself before anyone other than God is the vilest of vile deeds.

"After all, I did nothing but assume the very essence of justice. To those who asked me: 'Did you steal?' I answered: 'It is possible that I stole and equally possible that I did not.' Though such *true* answers are rare, the investigators did not appear at all mystified. They would laugh and offer me a cigarette, or else slap me or spit in my face (which, for them, is one and the same) . . .

"On the whole," Lichter reflected aloud, "one of the most dizzying abysses that has opened is between justice and morality. The very *formulas* which morality must breach in order to exist, triumph where justice is concerned: a pitiful, sinister triumph. Seeing it, I am sincerely tempted, if they insist on accusing me again, to declare myself a thief or a murderer rather than try to *appear* honest and dirty myself with the filth of false arguments. For I can *be* honest only before God . . .

"And besides," Lichter continued, "I felt that my soul was at ease among thieves, so much so that I would have become a martyr to the very idea of stealing with no regrets. Among modern myths few have more substance than that of the thief who gives to the poor.

"Just as between magnetic poles, there is great attraction between beggars and thieves. This explains why someone like me, who has assumed the profound vocation of begging, can swiftly and accurately understand the inner essence of thieves—from delicate, modest, almost virginal pickpockets to professional burglars or headstrong highway brigands. Rarely have I met anyone with a weaker sense of ownership than true thieves. For them *stealing* is simply one of the forms that revolt can take against *having*; thus, under certain conditions, stealing becomes an existential act. There are, of course, thieves that steal only to increase their possessions, for whom, in other words, the purpose, the essence of their acts is not stealing but *accumulating*. They are the ones who (if their honesty is called into question) usually manage to convince others they are telling the truth, and thus one rarely sees them serving time in prison. It's not of them that I speak, although they are the most numerous, but of those who, without declaring it, are filled, deep inside, with *pride* at being thieves (and chuckle with indulgent superiority when they are taken for something else): of those for whom stealing is a vocation."

And, letting himself be cradled by an utopian thought, Zacharias Lichter concluded: "I have long dreamed—an unattainable dream, yet so tenacious—of a massive social upheaval in which the majority of people become beggars. But now I realize that I must make room, in this grand revolution, for thieves as well. All will work voluntarily and without pay; in order to survive some will beg and others will steal. Ideally, beggars will seek alms from thieves, and thieves will steal from beggars. This is now my vision of the perfect citadel!"

# ON SELF-INDULGENCE

His puny figure, with its loose-jointed, erratic gestures, compels you to focus your attention first on his eyeglasses, which are so old and worn they appear to grow directly from the bridge of his nose. This impression is strengthened by the fact that one of the lenses is broken, a few sharp splinters still protruding from the frame. The other lens, though intact, is so darkened and speckled with dirt that the eye behind it appears lifeless, as though veiled by smoke. Ordinary wire, rusted by now, connects the eyeglass frames to the ears, twisting clumsily around them. T. the Great—as he likes to style himself, with obvious irony—never removes these vestiges of eyeglasses which, like the object of some strange cult, have long since lost their function and are now elevated to the rank of a symbol.

Unable to use the eye behind the broken lens, T. the Great orients himself in the world of the sighted as best he can with the other eye, its moist globe shielded by a wrinkled, hoary lid that blinks rapidly, creating the somewhat sickly and startled impression often found in the nearsighted. More so than the eyes, however, his ears have been disfigured by his obstinate decision to never remove his glasses. They are completely deformed by the wire wound about them and display old grooves long since rubbed raw, now scarred and rust-stained. His face is glabrous, imparting to it an uncomfortably juvenile look, though he is nearly forty. This impression, however, does not withstand closer scrutiny, for the rather dry skin of his cheeks is crisscrossed by a fine web of wrinkles.

A nimble and paradoxical spirit, T. the Great stands out from the bohemian society he frequents not only through his carefully crafted ugliness, but also by his bizarre penchant for self-disparagement. Whenever he talks about himself, he inflects his speech with accents that range from cruel irony to scorn and loathing, so that not even his fiercest (and cleverest) enemy can slander him more *artfully*. And truly, "art" is the most suitable word here, for the monstrous image T. the Great presents—or invents—for himself carries arcane and erudite aesthetic overtones. Even so, many think that the ambiguities of his behavior reflect an authentic inner conflict and indicate a nature tragically split. Nothing could be further from the truth, as we learn from Zacharias Lichter, who often encounters T. the Great in the various pubs he frequents in the company of Leopold Nacht.

"This man"—says Lichter—"hasn't tormented and disfigured himself in order to shed his individuality or to transcend it, but to impose it upon others. He represents the resentment of those who suffer from self-indulgence, who delight in transforming their fits of hysteria or frustration and their senseless minor tantrums into displays of universal anxiety. To someone like him, even the monstrous is simply an arena for self-indulgence and stimulating aesthetic pleasure. His behavior allows us insight into an inner tendency so mawkish and shameless it nauseates me—an otherwise unbearable feeling I can only dispel by transforming it into pity. His case, however, is not without interest. Viewed from a certain distance, calmly and dispassionately, it offers a perfect illustration of the strategy of self-indulgence. In general, we believe that those who enjoy being pampered aspire to comfort and luxury, which may be true on a superficial level. But those who suffer from more serious forms of the spiritual malady I call self-indulgence seek a more refined—and more distasteful—gratification in the tragic, the ugly, and the distorted . . . Thus hedonists find total gratification only in the pain of tragedy; the handsome, only in deformity; aristocrats, only in squalor and even begging. The result has been an aestheticizing of suffering, of ugliness, of poverty—an act which empties these states of all spiritual content and transforms them into simple rhetorical modes. Self-indulgence corrupts and belittles all that it touches. And, alas, when I look at the twisted and willfully grotesque figure of T. the Great I feel almost ashamed of my own ugliness. The longer I think about him, the more ashamed I am of my own suffering, and poverty, my most notable philosophical work, appears to me no more than a hollow word."

## ON LYING

"ONE WAY or another, all philosophical insight derives from an awareness of the mendacious nature of language"— Zacharias Lichter affirms. "In fact, in language, truth is always relative, partial, circumscribed—a fragment of a fragment, an echo of an echo, a mere shadow (hence the mind's tendency to create the most delicate and complex tools to capture and measure truth. What ingenuity in the elaboration of minor geometries! What squandering of thought!)

"That is why, in the world of words we inhabit (which the vampiric powers of language puncture and empty of reality), the supreme form of knowledge is silence. How profound is the Taoist meditation: 'The one who knows does not speak; the one who speaks does not know.' One and indivisible, truth is silent. It in-forms silence.

"But our fate is to talk, talk, talk without end—silence itself becomes a word like any other. We are left only with the clear recognition that we lie ceaselessly, that when we say something, 'we say what is not.' It is not just that we lie, but that *saying* lies to us, deforms us, denudes us of our being; that our emptiness ends in devastation and nonbeing; that we become a shelter for the void; that we die with every word we utter (and this death is a mockery of life, an absolute and icy irony against life).

"All we can do is be aware of this objective irony, whose

arctic coldness we cannot escape; to give this irony a dramatic sense; to ascend, not to knowledge but to philosophical insight, which is equivalent to participation in the drama of language.

"All that I say is a lie. *Yes* is a lie and *no* is a lie. Everything that can be said about anything is a lie. Ontologically speaking, there is no difference between calling God infinitely good and calling him a trash bin, a toothpick, or a rag; there is no difference even between saying God *is* and God *is not*.

"And, if we admit a hierarchy of lies, I, Zacharias Lichter, am the greatest lie of all: for my maxim is: *I lie*, therefore *I do not exist*. In that sense I draw near the devil. At times I even merge with him. What saves me, in the end, is the *nostalgia for truth*, a metaphysical nostalgia that fills my being with something divine, with timeless peace and ineffable joy.

"I cannot cast off the devil unless I pay the price of sharing his lying nature, of *taking on* his nonexistence ..."

# EULOGY OF THE QUESTION

"ANY QUESTION,"—Zacharias Lichter says—"no matter how innocent at first sight, probes the obscure density of language and is ultimately an indirect manifestation of the spirit's fundamental nostalgia for perplexity. Whoever asks a question truly, with his entire being, battles unknowingly for the triumph of the interrogative, striving to reach the point where no further answers are possible (or all are possible), where the mind floats, as in some natural medium, in the dark waters of perplexity. Viewed from this perspective, the stubborn and, to some, annoying manner in which children ask questions carries far more serious philosophical import than the way in which professional metaphysicians formulate their queries (technically refined so as to actually put us at our ease). After all, for professional thinkers, asking questions is merely a game, and one with fairly elementary rules at that (compared to which, for example, the rules of chess seem marvelously complex)—a game those trained to examine such matters with analytical rigor consider—to use a euphemism—quite puerile.

"Philosophers should accustom themselves to thinking in the presence of children. They should even try to become children again, to regain the lost vocation of asking. What they would learn first is that there are no objective criteria for establishing a hierarchy or taxonomy of questions: all questions, no matter how absurd, are equally justified; no distinction of value or nature among them is possible. A second important lesson philosophers would learn in proximity to children is that any question is part of an endless interrogative chain. In the dialectics of interrogation, the answer is only a means: its function is exclusively to generate a further question. The purpose of the interrogative process, irrespective of its practical content (with which, from the perspective of the infinite, it merges), is to facilitate the enactment of perplexity…

"Whoever asks himself or others a question in earnest"— Zacharias Lichter explains—"is not seeking an answer, but wishes to discover instead how that question might be inserted into the infinite interrogative chain. The answer is death, the question is life—in a purely spiritual sense, of course, and thus essentially dramatic. That is why, in spite of appearances, skeptics are thoroughly alien to the nature of the interrogative. They are dangerous corruptors, because they degrade questions by bestowing on them the function of answers, and *definitive* ones at that.

"I am always moved when revisiting a certain passage of the New Testament, in the Gospel according to John. When Jesus tells Pilate: 'Everyone that is of the truth heareth my voice,' Pilate, the skeptic par excellence, replies with a question-answer (as if this single question were self-sufficient): 'What is truth?' And the chapter ends with Christ's *silence*. Because of Christ's silence, Pilate's aesthetic-skeptical question becomes endless, reverberating forever through time: a trivial question that harbors the secret conceit of being *the answer* suddenly acquires a sublime resonance. Christ's silence at that moment is the deepest eulogy of questions ever given, because one can enter into perplexity only through the Gate of the Question.

"Likewise, we must learn from children"—Zacharias Lichter explains—"that silence is the supreme form of questioning: the moment at which the question questions itself and becomes perplexity.

"The mental evolution of humanity—which is nothing but the extension of the Realm of Stupidity—has led to a basic fear of questions. People have always tried to domesticate the question, to circumscribe it, to make it more sociable and even *useful*. The miracle of language has turned into a technique of 'pragmatic' answers. The most tenuous hypotheses have been invested with the prestige of realities (which can be replaced at any time with other 'more useful' realities); and, everywhere, so-called laws of progress have been put in motion by an increasingly perfidious betrayal of the original meaning of words.

"Words have grown rich, have gained weight, multiplied and settled, layer by layer, over the entire world, darkening it. From words arise the abscesses of all the demagogueries that render the air of time unbreathable, and truth itself has become just one more word among others.

"The spiritual fate of the word is solely to *embody the question*, so that the question, which is its being, may reveal itself. The word is fuel for the question's flame.

"Let us ask the world what children ask their parents: *why? why? why?*—endlessly, to exhaustion, and then causality will seem absurd.

"Let us ask the world: *how? how? how?*—endlessly, until modality becomes meaningless.

"Let us ask the world: *when? when? when?*—until time unveils its essential unreality.

"Let us ask the world: *where? where? where?*—and enter the paradox of spatiality.

"To be saved, we must follow to the end (an endless end) all the questions we can think of, from the most naive to the most complex and abstract, without favoring one over another, with equal humility before all, because all roads that open under the aegis of the interrogative, if persistently followed, lead to one and the same place, a place where there are no words, a place filled with truth."

# ON IMAGINATION

FOR A WHILE, like a night butterfly, an aging apprentice of sorts revolved around the incandescent being of Zacharias Lichter. In fact, he had graduated in the Humanities but continued to register for classes in one or two other departments, firmly determined not to repeat his earlier error of seeing all his courses through to the end: for his true vocation was that of the "eternal student." He was in fact an adult who tried by all possible means to prolong a rather artificial adolescence consisting of ecstatic exclamations, vague flowing gestures, a seraphic frankness, and a sweet, harmless, and persistently silly air of distraction. He walked with a light skipping motion vaguely reminiscent of ballet steps but in an imperfect rhythm, with sudden ungainly movements. At times he would stumble deliberately, for no apparent reason, as if he had bumped into some invisible object, and then peer in vain on all sides, ahead, behind, to the right, to the left, his eyes wide in amazement.

He enjoyed, especially during evening hours, roaming through the busiest streets while whistling airs from Mozart, arias from the *Zauberflöte*, from *Don Giovanni*, from *Così fan tutte*, and also, at times, themes more difficult to memorize, from symphonies or sonatas—and always only by Mozart, whose name he could not say or hear without some word of enthusiasm uttered in a squeal that rendered it barely decipherable. As a matter of fact, Anselmus—that's what everyone called him, for he declared himself, openly and with utmost gravity, to be an avatar of Hoffmann's character of that name in *Der goldne Topf*—expressed his appreciation of everything in this way, whenever the occasion arose. And not only his appreciation. His scale of values could be reconstructed with sufficient precision from the intensity and types of sounds he emitted, to the surprise, embarrassment, and even alarm of those not forewarned: from an elevated squeal that was almost intolerable to delicate ears (reserved for immortal works) to a more moderate one (for works of primarily historical merit), to low yet no less suggestive tones of loathing and abhorrence that, bypassing his strong vocal cords, emerged as muffled puffs, snorts and similar guttural rumbles, the main expressive role having now been assigned to scowls and grimaces.

Just as with his real name, which he never used and only a handful knew, few had knowledge of even the skimpiest biographical details about Anselmus (at least any that were plausible). This despite his readiness to talk about himself in a confessional tone with anyone willing to listen. Anselmus's confessions were so obviously the fabulations of a mythomaniac ruled by fantasy that it was impossible to discern, within the texture of their steadily shifting waters, even the slightest fact or detail worthy of credence. The whole had an air of endless babble. You could easily believe you were being made fun of had not Anselmus instilled his confessions with a strange, obscure, and oddly thrilling persuasiveness. Imperceptibly, a sort of a game would be instituted in which he pretended to believe in the follies he poured forth, forcing you to pretend, in turn, that you were taking them seriously. But only *pretend*, nothing more. At first the situation seemed comical, and you might even start to enjoy it; but soon the humor faded and the game—since you had already agreed to play it—gripped you more forcefully. Not that you actually believed what he said, but you realized with increasing clarity that adopting the normal criteria of credibility would be pointless, misguided even, since this would compromise the normal course of the game: its charm lay in the pretense itself. In the end you no longer played the game, strictly speaking, but only played at it.

The more absurd and incredible Anselmus's tales became the more you were impelled by some hidden force to look increasingly convinced, to provide a more intense, though consciously *mimed*, participation. Thus, if you made friends with Anselmus, you might easily end up pretending to take all he said at face value, as indisputably true as daylight is for those who can see. Heartened, looking you straight in the eye and speaking in a voice that ranged up and down the scale, changing musical keys as in a recitative, Anselmus would evoke for hours on end nostalgic recollections of his childhood years, spent in a gigantic tree inhabited by 1,217 birds, whose species he could describe in detail, including both their appearance and their strange behavior. He had been left in this tree, not yet a year old, by some wretched relative who did not wish to be burdened with an orphan child. But an orphan only briefly, since Anselmus would also discourse at length on the subject of his father, a former navigator and explorer, who was living out the final years of his stormy life in some unknown locale. From this father (he had others as well, who had passed on various other character traits and habits) he had inherited a taste for travel and adventure. (Among the tales he told was one that constantly reappeared with only small variants, about a Robinsonian shipwreck and the ingenious way he had escaped the deserted island by taming a giant eagle—benefitting from his childhood years among the birds—which carried him to the balcony of his upper-floor studio in an apartment building on Sapienza Street.) From other accounts it seems he had been reared by an uncle who was a salamander (an obvious Hoffmannian echo) toward the end of the eighteenth century and could not imagine how he had landed in the present epoch, towards which he felt nothing but hostility. Unfolding and whirling his romantic imaginary cloak about him from morn to night, Anselmus never tired of playing this bizarre character, incompetent and hilarious, in whom many people found a peculiar charm.

In fact, what Anselmus sought was to *seem*: to seem for the sake of seeming, with no practical aim in mind. Willfully farfetched and bewildering, his stories nonetheless aspired toward credibility of a special nature, perched at the very edge of the imaginary. A credibility which, once its rules were accepted, might produce a fissure, a tiny crack in the banal and uniform surface of reality through which one could glimpse the mirages of the imagination, the pure games of make-believe seeking only to be make-believe.

One of his friends claimed Anselmus had confessed, some years ago, his desire to develop a "pedagogy of beguilement." Seen in this light, the behavior of this "eternal student," which at first sight might appear confused, gains a certain inner logic. Beguilement—Anselmus appears to believe—attains its consummate form only when it recognizes openly that it is only beguilement. In other words, it no longer deceives anyone, in the practical sense (and no longer risks becoming, even involuntarily, *imposture*). At that stage, that-which-beguiles no longer *seems to be* but, purely and simply, *seems*. (To seem becomes, in the strictest sense, a category.)

We can see that Anselmus—consistent to the end—was driven by the secret desire not to seem to be one thing or the other (as one might mistakenly suspect) but to-be-in-order-to-seem. Thus seeming became for him the goal and supreme value of existence.

In the beginning, Zacharias Lichter had been amazed and to some extent (if ever so slightly) captivated by the charm of the fluttering apparition of this "butterfly man," whose large and delicate wings were forever changing hues and nuances. This time, the prophet had allowed himself, humanly—all too humanly, to be duped by appearances. Not long after, however, when he heard that Anselmus had developed a great admiration for him (he always accompanied Lichter's name with his well-known superlatives, those exalted cries reserved exclusively for immortal personages and works), Zacharias Lichter was seized by an indignation he could barely curb. For him, Anselmus had become the embodiment (in a picturesque, degraded form) of the *irresponsibility and misery of imagination*.

"The 'freer' and 'purer' the imagination is"—Zacharias Lichter declared—"the dirtier, the filthier, the more imbued with the debris and refuse of resentment it becomes. To the clear-sighted, its soaring flight cannot mask, beneath the unstable brilliance of false glamour, a repugnant, hideous wretchedness.

"Up to a point, so long as it subordinates itself naturally and humbly to moral imperatives, we must admit that imagination is one of the means by which our fundamental nostalgia for *being* expresses itself. One might say it is even creative, but only within the confines of this nostalgia, which it can amplify and intensify, which it can 'dramatize.' As a mimetic force, imagination can also play a compensatory role, tending to balance the functions of the psychological mechanisms of *desire* and to instill a certain harmony in the interplay of their contradictory aims.

"But imagination can also be used—hence its danger—beyond its natural borders; it can be, and often is, used to serve resentment, both in its elementary and in its more complex and highly developed forms. It is here that it finds deployment (a most noxious one) in its subtle capacity to falsify and to counterfeit, not in order to fulfill a need but to undermine and destroy *reality* itself in one or another of its aspects. With all its protean powers, imagination is apt to turn—and this can happen at any time—into an instrument of *resentment against being*, into an instrument of vengeance. True, the terrible resentment of which I am speaking"—and one could read sheer horror and fear in Lichter's face—"most often chooses to manifest itself by *way of possession*, the slow yet sure progression into the sphere of *having*. (Thus was born the Realm of Stupidity, where imagination is forced to content itself with a rather humiliating ancillary position, its role confined to that of mere amusement.) But if aided by an out-of-the-ordinary imagination, resentment against being may also achieve full satisfaction in the sphere of *seeming*. Having achieved the status of a category, seeming may appropriate the ineffable attributes of being and place the latter under its total dominion.

"Imagination thus seems to us, in its essence, a *possible* means of dematerializing, of devastating being—albeit a means illustrated at the level of caricature and buffoonery in the abject figure of Anselmus. Yes, abject, in the deepest meaning of the word"—Zacharias Lichter became heated—"for although his imagination remains mediocre (and fortunately so), his resentment against being is as deep as that of the worst monsters of having... In a sense, difficult as it is to believe, the dangers of *seeming* are potentially greater than even those of *having*. Who knows what would happen to us, large and small alike, enraptured by the spirit and burnt by the divine flame, if an Anselmus or someone of his ilk, *just one*, possessed a truly rich imagination? Because, freed from the fetters of responsibility, imagination knows no measure or bounds, filled as it is by overweening pride in its own ability to craft anything it wishes to and, above all, at being able to invent *itself* as pure seeming, as both the being and nonbeing of seeming.

"The fact that until now the resentment of all resentment has chosen the more comfortable road of *having* does not mean in the least that it may not, once all necessary conditions are met, embark on the road of *seeming*. Then an Anselmus could transform the entire world, as if at the stroke of a magic wand, into a vast game of words and illusions. The Realm of Stupidity would be wiped from the face of the earth but, alas, only to be replaced by another empire, even more odious, the Realm of Seeming. You, I, and all who exist would cease to *be*—we would find ourselves struggling for all eternity in a thousand-faced void spawned by the imagination of some Anselmus..."

# THE MORAL LAW

THE MORAL law—Zacharias Lichter believes—is given to us neither to be respected nor to be infringed, but above all simply to be *law*: the criterion of criteria, the pure core out of which arise, like emanations, the possibilities of fulfilling or defiling it. Its essence is one with its ideal form. People are not, in practice, "moral" or "immoral." Before the *law* we are all immoral in an absolute sense, and the supreme moral act is the consciousness of this state, with endless anguish as its inescapable consequence.

To uphold or deny the law is a purely theoretical option, having nothing to do with life as it flows, irreversibly, through ever-changing words.

Moral law can only be *recognized*, and that through a perilous mental illumination that may blind the spirit. It can even be *understood* in its terrifying abstraction, through a kind of grace. But to *apply* it is impossible.

Impossible because, when applied, the law alienates itself from its essence; because the results of its "application" can only *invoke* (but not embody) the law, can only empty it of its substance, reducing it to the state of a name that may name anything.

Every law is fierce; the moral law is the fiercest of all: more severe than the gaze of angels; clearer and more frightening in its silent inflexibility; harsher: it does not forgive and does not punish; more inhuman, because it is the source of our freedom to be anywhere except near to it.

As human beings we are condemned to strive to fulfill the law but, alas!, without the right to affirm our submission or nonsubmission to it. Because in either case we would merely falsify it, complying with or rejecting not the law itself, but its phantasm, an illusory shadow.

We are given only a few *rules*, some more or less autonomous systems of rules. Consciously or not, we choose those pertaining to the *game* we want to or are able to play.

But the thorny and barren path that leads to the law begins only when the game is denied by the very rigor with which we respect its rules: and this is a modality of *irony*.

Consciousness of the law implies the destructive work of irony.

Verily, the law reveals itself only to those who, through irony, discover its absence from all systems of rules (whatever their pretenses).

That is all that can be said about the Law.

# FROM THE POEMS OF ZACHARIAS LICHTER

## CARDINAL POINTS

Fractured gears of Ecstasy
at sunset white pyres at sunrise
     at midnight
     at midday
over the sun's eye a chalk lid
from the void's merry-go-round scream the nameless ill
dwarves with huge heads turn somersaults in dust
cripples blow into old trumpets like angels
but for us time is ever scarcer
more traceless than the arrow of the scream
than the somersaults of dwarves in wind-scattered dust
than the trumpets' ta-ra-ra
more self-less than each
of our own selves
more sense-less
than the fair with snake-women and ancient clowns
time ever closer to no-time and to no-love
with sun's eye snuffed out beneath the chalk lid
with monsters who wish to make us laugh
or cry and forget

the fractured gears of Ecstasy
at sunset the white pyres at sunrise
     at midnight
     and at midday.

# EPILOGUE: ZACHARIAS LICHTER AND HIS BIOGRAPHER

"I THOUGHT you loved me"—Zacharias Lichter once said to his would-be biographer, having just learned of his project. "But in fact you only love yourself, for you are writing about yourself, not me. You put yourself in my stead, like the liar and the nonentity you are, for you wish to rediscover in me your own misery and weakness, to ennoble them, to bathe them in the burning, barren atmosphere surrounding my being.

"You are worthless: a worm, a traitor, a criminal. But I do not fear you! For in mocking me, you mock yourself. Spattering me with dirt, you spatter yourself. Denying me, you deny yourself.

"And now, may I ask what moved you to write my biography? Don't you see that my 'biography' is the last thing that could possibly be written? If I knew, at least, that you meant to write a fictional life of Zacharias Lichter, so be it! Or a comedic history, serene, Don-Quixotic, naive, larger than life. Unfortunately, however, you suffer from the malady of serious-mindedness. You carefully avoid all ordinary emotions and find laughter vulgar. I predict that the biography you write will be serious and boring, cold, perhaps awkwardly ironic; something fitting only for yourself. Yet I have no right to prevent you. In fact, as you write about yourself, you may eventually manage to understand some small part of me. Then you will despise yourself, you will disown yourself, and perhaps you will feel in your estranged flesh, now icy and dying, the scorching heat of God's flame."

The one who had set about recording the life and opinions of Zacharias Lichter realized he could no longer continue. He felt ashamed. He understood that he had betrayed his hero and in doing so betrayed himself. He understood that for the prophet—though Lichter seemed unaware of this— his book posed an even greater danger than Doctor S.'s monstrous desire to analyze him—that it deprived him of his final chance to free himself from the dreadful prison of signification. And since he loved Zacharias Lichter a terrible sadness, an icy regret settled upon his soul, a sense of having done something irreparable.

Lichter's face had become almost transparent.

"All that being said"—he resumed in a calmer tone of voice—"and to be consistent, I should also be grateful to you. No matter what you write in your book, the simple fact of its existence obliges me to face my own failure, and even my own death . . ."

Lichter's biographer wondered inwardly if he should burn his manuscript. As if guessing his thoughts, Lichter addressed him in a voice that seemed to come from great distance: "Once things have reached this point, there is nothing to be done. Your book will exist, even if no one reads it, even if you burn it. Your sin was to *write* it, my sin to inspire it—and such sins cannot be erased. They can only be acknowledged, in pain and fear. And this acknowledgment will only take place when I become you and you become me, at the moment I set about writing your biography. And although I have not read a thing you've written about me, I am sure that what I will write *then* about you will be identical: word for word. A book in which God's flame itself, instead of burning, will freeze all things it touches."

# OTHER NEW YORK REVIEW CLASSICS

*For a complete list of titles, visit www.nyrb.com or write to:*
*Catalog Requests, NYRB, 435 Hudson Street, New York, NY 10014*

* *Also available as an electronic book.*